BEAUTIFUL MONSTERS

Beautiful Monsters

a Jen Rice novel

SHANON L. MAYER

Shanon L. Mayer

Books by Shanon L. Mayer

<u>Chronicles of the Chosen</u>
Sphere of Power
Veil of Deception
Reflections of Doubt

<u>Jen Rice novels</u>
Captives and Prisoners
Festival of Souls
Beautiful Monsters

<u>Inland Sea</u>
Star of Darkness
Eyes of Midnight

For Connie, Aaron, Patti, and Jesse.

Thanks for supporting me through all
of my meltdowns!

Chapter 1

It was well past noon when David Melrose, Director of New World Response, walked into his office. There was already a mountain of files in his inbox and he didn't want to know how many voice messages were waiting for him. The light on his phone was blinking enough to assure him that there were more than enough to keep him occupied for the rest of the day, if he dealt with all of them right now. Not that he had any intention of responding to all of them but there were bound to be at least a few that required immediate attention, he realized with a frown. He wasn't usually late getting to work but the last week had been rough on everyone.

David was a large man and his years of law enforcement showed in every line that creased his forehead. His blue eyes were bloodshot and slightly clouded from sleep deprivation, even his lukewarm morning shower hadn't quite been enough to bring him back to his normal state of readiness. What he really needed was another six or seven hours of sleep but that wasn't going to be forthcoming any time soon.

He took off his overcoat and hung it on its customary hook on the back of his door and glared out the large window behind his desk. The rain had finally gotten cold enough to turn to sleet and the weather forecasters were predicting snow by the beginning of next week. If this was any other year, he would be looking forward to a good snowfall but he had far too much to do before he could hit the slopes this year. His annual ski trip would just have to wait.

As he sat down at his desk, he glanced over the pile of old reports that littered his desk. He had been too tired the night before to organize his files and put them away before heading home like he normally would have done. With a sigh, he began gathering up the loose papers and putting them into their folders. Just because he was tired, that didn't mean he had to turn into a slob.

One of the papers in particular caught his attention as he shuffled through them. A report filed almost two weeks before by his newest officer, the page outlined a conversation she'd had with a confidential person, who she had only referred to as a friend, about his missing daughter. David remembered that his officer had mentioned that her friend was a vampire and he turned to his computer to run a search of the registered vampires in the area. Maybe, after having had a mediocre night's sleep, he would be able to uncover something that hadn't already been found.

He wasn't looking out of curiosity. As far as David was concerned, it didn't matter who or what her friend was or whether or not her vampiric friend was legally registered. What had his attention was the fact that the agent he had been talking to, who had agreed to take on the search for his missing daughter, had gone missing herself during her investigation and the vampire might have information about where she had been taken. Maybe, he mused without much enthusiasm, the vampire might even have an idea of how to get her back.

Jen Rice had only worked for New World Response for just under two months at the time she disappeared but in those two months she had created quite a stir in the paranormal investigation community. Her killer instincts and fearless attitude had led her to uncover some of the most surprising, not to mention dangerous, activities that David could have thought of. Even the National Paranormal Investigative Board, or NPIB, had recently become interested in her because of her success rate.

The NPIB was the monitoring agency that oversaw all of the paranormal activity throughout the country, responsible for issuing licenses to response teams and certifications to response team members. For someone to even be considered for a position in the NPIB, it usually took a respected military career, years in law enforcement, and personal recommendation by a senior staff member. Jen had none of those but her actions during her brief career with New World had been more than impressive.

Now David had one of the staff analysts from

the NPIB breathing down his neck, wanting to know when he and some of his NPIB agents would be able to meet with Jen and David didn't know what to tell him. It wasn't exactly like he could just tell them that the person they were here to meet with had been kidnapped by a demon, that wasn't likely to be an easily accepted response. He wasn't sure how long he could continue putting off the inevitable.

His computer beeped, signaling that his search was complete. He turned to the monitor and swore as he saw how many registered vampires lived in the area. He narrowed the search to only registered vampires who had at least one female child and ran the search again. He doubted that the advanced search would turn up much; the child in question had lived a hundred years ago and there was little chance that she would be listed in the database but he had to narrow the search somehow. For now, it was all he had.

While he waited for the search to finish, he clicked over to the building's security system. He had to put in his personal override code in order to access the video feed he sought, one that allowed him to view the holding cell in the sub-basement where the only prisoner that New World Response currently held remained captive. Once his authorization code was processed and accepted, the image of a beautiful woman appeared on the screen, the dark and dreary cell not detracting from her otherworldly beauty in the slightest. Although she had been in the same cell for over a week, her hair still held its luster and her clothes still appeared as fresh and new as they had the day she had been brought in.

Initially, David had been worried about checking in on the woman, even distantly through the video camera and monitor, but he had quickly discovered that the security system was the best way to keep tabs on her. No men were allowed in the sub-basement while she was held there, for good reason. The last time that particular woman had been in direct contact with the men from the response unit, the same day she had been captured, the prisoner had used a mind-altering ability to force the men in the unit to turn against one of their own teammates.

After almost killing her, he amended the thought. Her powers useless against the only female member of the team, the demoness had forced the rest of the team to capture Jen and had in fact forced them to turn her over to another demon before her mental domination over the response team had been broken.

As he watched, the door to the demon's cell opened. A short, red-haired woman, on loan from the local police department and still wearing the police-issue navy blue uniform, stepped into the cell to perform the standard visual confirmation. David wasn't willing to take any chances on the demon escaping so he had required physical checks every eight hours to verify that the demoness was still in her cell. Since Jen had been the only female response team member on staff at the time of the demon's capture, David had needed to call in a few favors to borrow a rookie police officer.

Once the verification check was complete, David switched his monitor back to check on his search for Jen's vampire and swore. "How can there be so many vampires with kids?" he asked as he saw that there were still over a hundred in the local community. "I thought vampires were supposed to be sterile." To an outside observer, David's expression might have appeared bleak, even hopeless, but he was determined to succeed in this no matter how long it took. In his opinion, finding Jen had already taken far longer than it should have and every day just served to make the matter worse.

Before he could figure out how to narrow the search further, his fax machine started to click and hum, breaking the sullen silence of the office. With a groan, he turned to see what was coming down the line this time. He knew that whatever the fax was, it couldn't be good but he also knew that it was his own fault. He hadn't reported that Jen was missing and, because of that, the NPIB had no reason to believe that the New World team wasn't operating at full capacity.

He snatched the paper out of the machine and headed for the stairs.

The fact that his team was one person short wasn't the only concern that David had about letting his men go out into the field. They had all been in a thoroughly rotten mood for the last week and he couldn't blame them. They all felt responsible for losing Jen, even though they rationally understood that none of them were at fault over what had befallen her. David just hoped that they wouldn't go too overboard on their latest assignment. He prided himself on having an honest, upstanding team and didn't want the NPIB to have any reason to cut their support. Or their funding.

When he arrived in the team's meeting room, he wasn't surprised to see all of them waiting there. The members of the response team had spent most of their time in the training rooms over the last week, working through the stress and brainstorming for ideas on how to get Jen back. So far, none of them had managed to come up with a workable plan but thankfully they weren't the only ones working on it. The down side was that they had made about as much progress in the search for Jen as everyone else had. As one, they turned hopeful eyes toward David as he stepped purposefully into the room.

Marc Anderson, the unit leader, was the first one to stand and approach him. "Have you found anything?" he asked. Marc was only barely six feet tall, with light brown hair and eyes that had lost some of their luster as his anxiety had grown over the last week. Now, with the hope of news about Jen, they momentarily brightened.

David shook his head. "Not about Jen." He held up the orders that had been faxed in and Marc's face fell. "But you have an assignment."

"How can anyone expect us to go out now?" Ty Williams was the tallest member of the group, with dark skin and eyes. Although he usually kept his head cleanly shaved, there was a few days' worth of stubble showing. "We don't have the whole team."

J.J. Monroe agreed with Ty. "We've done it before, I know, but you can't just expect us to go out there like she'd never been here." J.J. was a tall blonde with blue eyes and had been one of Jen's closest friends in the group. David had expected some resistance from J.J. but he hadn't expected this much hesitation from everyone else, too.

Mike Brown, a little bigger than Marc, had finally trimmed his beard back down to a reasonable length. Now, it looked more like a soul patch than the goatee he had been sporting for the last few months. Surprisingly, he was the voice of reason. He turned to the rest of the group and held up a hand. "Look, everyone misses Jen and I don't think I'm the only one who only wants to go out and find her. But we still have a job to do and we can't just sit here on our asses and wait for her to come back." He looked back over at David. "Just tell me it's not another damned demon, I don't think any of us can handle one of those right now."

David shook his head. "No, this one's a vampire. Looks like he went into a blood rage last night." He stepped over to Marc and handed him the paperwork.

When a vampire went for too long between feedings, the hunger for blood could overtake their actions, putting them into a frenzy that didn't subside until the vampire had fed, usually on more than one victim. It was because of this rage that a law had been passed regarding their access to food. All a vampire had to do, whether it was legally registered or not, was walk into a blood bank and say that he was hungry. Every bank in the country was required to keep an amount of blood on hand for just such an occurrence and there were even a handful of blood banks that were open all night.

The law had worked as intended and vampire attacks decreased rapidly once the vampire population had access to food that they didn't have to kill for. However, there were still the occasional cases where either a vampire wasn't able to make it to a blood bank or, less often, had decided that it preferred its meal fresh. These instances were the most common types of vampire activity that the response teams would get called into action for.

Marc flipped through the fax. "Is this a capture order, or a kill one?" Most of New World's orders were capture orders, where they just had to go out and apprehend the offender. The only real difficulty in those assignments was locating their targets, which were usually aware that there was a team after them and were hiding.

This paperwork looked a little different from the norm.

"This Vamp's already killed five, two of which have changed," David explained. While it wasn't illegal to be a vampire, or to become one, it was highly illegal to create one. The survival rate of the transformation was minuscule, low enough that the courts had decided fairly quickly that it shouldn't be allowed. Therefore, even changing a willing person into a vampire was an automatic death sentence for the vampire if they were caught.

"Do we know what set him off?" Marc asked. "Was it just hunger, or is this guy wanting to kill"

David shook his head again. "We don't really have a lot of information on what happened. The report I got said that his first victim was before sundown, unusual for a Vamp. He probably has some pretty bad burns because the rest of his victims were in places outside his house, which means he had to have gone out in the sunlight."

Unlike in the movies, where a vampire would burst into flame and disintegrate as soon as it came into contact with sunlight, real vampires didn't catch fire. They reacted just as a regular human would if they were out in the sun for too long and they suffered from second- and third-degree burns much more quickly than humans did.

"What about sun block?" Ty asked. "Could he have used some to go out in the daytime?"

"Possible but unlikely," David answered. "There are only a couple of shops in town that sell vampire-strength sun block and it's expensive as hell. Even if he did have some, I doubt that a raging Vamp is going to remember to slather on the protection before going out to continue his rampage."

"So do we know where he is?" Marc asked, "Or do we get to go look for him?"

"We have an idea of where he is." David indicated the report that Marc was still flipping through. "The last time he was spotted was just outside the downtown district, that sighting was only a few hours ago. As of right now, we're thinking that he's on his way back home, so the idea is for you to wait for him there." He checked his watch. "He's been out and about for almost eighteen hours now, so he'll need to get back to his safe zone to rest before too much longer."

"If he's out now, then he's going to be

pretty desperate to get home." Outside, the sun wasn't particularly strong because of the onset of winter but there was still more than enough light to seriously hurt an unprotected vampire. Marc closed the report and tucked it under an arm as he stood. "Let's go get him, then. There shouldn't be too much involved here, it's hard to miss a burning Vamp at two in the after-noon."

The rest of the team reluctantly stood up and followed him to the lockers to gear up. David watched them for a moment before head-ing back to the elevator. Even though it looked like a fairly basic assignment, he hoped that the team could hold it together enough to get it done. Nobody knew better than he exactly how much hell his team was going through right now.

More than that, he hoped that they didn't go overboard but he could hardly blame them if they did.

He stepped onto the elevator and pressed the button for the third floor, intent on run-ning another search as soon as he got back to his office. This time, instead of looking for Jen's vampire, who wasn't all that likely to know anything about where Jen had been taken even if David could narrow the search to find the right vampire in the haystack of results, he was going to see if the NPIB had any new information on demons. After all, if the demon activity that the New World team had been encountering was any indication of how many encounters other response teams across the country had been having, they were bound to have something on file about them. Although demonic activity was rare, New World couldn't be the only ones that had been dealing with the bastards.

David hadn't ever heard of a demon with mind tricks like the one they held downstairs had but if the NPIB had a record of something similar, it might give them something concrete to go from, or at the very least a lead they hadn't already beaten to exhaustion. Even if the Board only had the barest of details, it would still be a lot more than the team had now.

Before he got to his office, however, he was interrupted by his phone. "Sir, the hybrid's here again, trying to get into the holding cell." Theodora Michaels, the borrowed police officer guarding the demoness, had been having trouble with Troy Franklin since the demon had been brought in. At least once a day, Troy had been caught trying to get past the security to interrogate the demoness and Theo was clearly getting tired of it. "I have him stopped just outside the danger zone; can I have him removed?"

David sighed. "No, I'm on my way. Just keep him there until I get there." Troy had been Jen's friend and part-time bodyguard, sent by a couple of her friends for her protection. For the most part he had been effective, keeping her alive through a previous demonic attack and helping her to thwart a handful of assassination attempts. Because of that, it wasn't much of a surprise that Troy was desperate to get to the demoness.

Beyond that, Troy had been involved in a few cases where the New World team had responded. When he had first considered building a second team for New World, David had briefly considered offering Troy a job but the hybrid was unpredictable and had a record of problems with authority. The most that David would be willing to offer was a consulting position but he wasn't sure about even that much. Though his services and assistance had been valuable in the past, David still wasn't ready to take the next leap with Troy.

Nor was he ready to completely dismiss the idea, either.

Most hybrids, offspring of a werewolf and a human, developed moderate to severe behavioral issues and Troy was no exception. When David had first considered offering the hybrid a position on the team, he had run a full background check. Troy had been enlisted in the military for a period of years before his commander had sent him for a psychological evaluation for "erratic behavior" and the psychologist had refused to let him back into the field. This type of concern wasn't all that uncommon with hybrids so it was an honorable discharge but David was still hesitant about having Troy underfoot too often. In his experience, erratic behavior tended to lead to fatalities and he had known Troy long enough now to recognize that the psychological evaluation was a valid one.

When David got to the sub-basement where the demoness was housed, he was met by a sight that made even him stop and gape, slack-jawed and speechless.

Troy was hanging from one of the security lights, about five feet up the side wall of the hallway. Both of his feet were on the wall and he was busily wrenching on the fixture as though he was trying to rip it from its bracket. The chain that connected his belt to the wallet in his rear pocket rattled almost as furiously as the light fixture as he struggled against the wall.

Theo was on the ground behind him, holding an enormous pistol, which looked even larger in her small hands. She held it aimed towards the ground but David knew that she could raise and fire it without warning. She didn't take her eyes off Troy but nodded toward David as though to acknowledge his presence. "Hiya boss," she said calmly.

Once he had regained his composure, David looked between the pair, from Troy to Theo and back to Troy again. "What the hell is going on here?" Though his voice was as stern as usual, it was a struggle to maintain a straight face and not burst into laughter. Of all the sights he could have witnessed, he knew that this one would live in his memory for months to come.

Theo shrugged in response. "You told me to keep him here." The gun wavered slightly as her shoulders moved and David hoped that she didn't accidentally discharge the weapon. He wasn't sure how he would be able to explain the wound if there was an inquiry.

With a sigh, he called over to Troy. "Get down before you break that thing." The metal of the light had come loose as Troy wrenched on it, so there was a very real chance that the whole fixture would come crashing down to the ground, hybrid included.

"Can't," Troy grunted in response. The metal groaned again as he tugged.

"Why not?"

Troy shuffled sideways enough for David to see that one of his feet had been shackled to the light. "I can't get to my key," he explained. A single knee peered through the hybrid's jeans and David wondered whether the tear had happened in the struggle or if Troy had already been wearing damaged pants when he arrived.

David stared at the cuffs in astonishment. "How did your foot get attached to that?"

"He tried to kick me," Theo explained, "and I didn't really feel like playing today."

David slowly nodded. "For starters, how about you let him down?"

Theo tucked the pistol into her waistband and moved to unlock her captive. Troy kept his eyes locked on her movements until he was released. Once he was free, he dropped to the floor and rubbed his sore legs. "Can I have my gun back?"

David looked down at the pistol that still sat in Theo's belt. "Is that his?"

"He had it in the back of his pants. I figured it'd be best if I just held on to it for a while."

"Well, I don't think he's going to be using it, so go ahead and give it back." When she handed it over, David noticed the teeth prints in Troy's right hand. "What happened?"

Theo shrugged as Troy glared at her. "He tried to stop me from taking the gun, so I bit him." She looked concerned for a moment. "You don't think he has rabies, do you?"

She smiled sweetly as Troy sputtered. David

decided that it was a good time to get Troy out of there, so he took him by an arm and led him towards the elevator. "Why do you keep doing this?"

"Bitch won't answer you guys, so I figured I'd have a talk with her."

David shook his head. "I meant, why do you keep coming down here and antagonizing Theo like that?"

"Oh, that." As they stepped into the elevator, Troy slipped the pistol into the holster in the back of his jeans. "Because it's fun, I guess."

"Fun?"

"Well, yeah." Troy looked over at him. "For one, Theo's hot and there's something awesome about those little redheads. They've got fire in their veins, you know. Plus, there's the fact that she's good, so there's a challenge when I go down there. It's not like training with the guys because she's a lot meaner than they are and I can burn off some energy. And if I do manage to get past her, I get to the demon bitch, so it's all good."

David shook his head. "You know why we can't let you get to her."

"Come on," Troy protested. "I'm one of the only people that was able to get out of her spell, remember?"

David remembered very well. When the demoness had handed Jen over to be taken away, Troy and Joel, another hybrid and friend of Jen's, had managed to break free of her mental hold. "But it took you hitting rage to get out of it, didn't it?"

Troy shrugged noncommittally as he scratched at his beard. "I got out once, I can get out again."

"Let's not take that chance, shall we? We'll call you as soon as we know anything. I give you my word." As the elevator doors opened, David watched Troy to make sure he left the building. As the hybrid walked out the front door, David stepped back into the elevator and rode the rest of the way to his office.

He hadn't been expecting any visitors that day, nor did he have any meetings scheduled, so he was surprised to see someone waiting in his office when he arrived. A man with short, well-kept dark brown hair, brown eyes, and not even a hint of stubble sat quietly in a chair in front of David's desk. He was dressed in a charcoal grey suit and a blue tie and David winced when he saw his shoes. Those alone would cost a month of David's pay. People wearing expensive shoes always meant bad news and the more expensive the shoes were, the worse news they walked in with.

As David walked across the room, the man stood and offered a hand. "Charlie Winters, NPIB. I believe we've spoken on the phone."

David took his hand. "Sorry, I hadn't been expecting you. Did we have an appointment?" His initial assessment had been correct. Those were some of the most expensive shoes he had seen in a long time.

"No," Charlie shook his head. "I was in the area on other business and I figured I'd drop in to talk with you. If this is a bad time, I can come back later."

"No, it's not a bad time." David sat in his chair. "How can I help you?"

"I was hoping to talk with you about one of your employees, Jennifer Rice. I have been trying to get in touch with her for the last few days but I haven't been able to speak with her yet." Charlie smiled across the desk at David. "I don't suppose she's here now, is she?"

David closed his eyes and sighed. Of everything that could happen right then, this was about the least he had wanted to deal with. He pinched the bridge of his nose and looked back at Charlie. "I'm afraid she isn't here at the moment."

"Out on assignment, I assume?"

"Could I ask why you are looking for Jen?" David knew perfectly well why he was looking for her but he needed to stall and give himself a moment to try and figure out how to get out of this mess without telling Charlie what was really going on and why Jen was out of contact.

"Of course. My office has recently gotten a number of reports about Ms. Rice and we like what we are hearing. She seems to have a talent for getting beneath the surface of things and we were hoping to be able to speak with her and see if our in-person impressions match what we've seen on paper."

David sighed. He had hoped to keep the NPIB out of the mess for a little bit longer but there was an enormous difference between avoiding their phone calls and lying to one of their officers in person. He folded his hands on his desk and lowered his head. "I'm afraid that won't be possible at the moment."

"Why is that?" Charlie's smile faded, and he was clearly growing irritated with the situation. "Look, the only reason I'm here is to talk with her. I have tried calling her at her house but the people who answer her phone have refused to let her speak to me. If she isn't interested in a position with us, all she has to do is say so. I'm not here to force her into anything that she doesn't want to do.

"But the fact remains that whether we decide to offer her a position or not and whether she accepts or denies it if we do is beside the point. Despite whatever may happen, I do need to speak with her."

"I understand that," David admitted. "But that doesn't change the fact that you can't speak with her right now."

"And why not?" Charlie leaned forward in his chair as he asked.

"Because we don't know where she is."

Stunned by David's admission, Charlie sat back again. "What do you mean?"

"She was kidnapped while on mission not long ago and we've been trying to find her since then."

"When was she taken?" Charlie asked. "I didn't get any reports on that."

"I know." David slumped in his seat, ever so slightly. "She was helping a friend retrieve his daughter, who had been kidnapped. In the process of that, she was taken herself."

"How long has she been missing?"

"Just shy of a week," David admitted. Even as he answered, he could barely believe the words he was speaking. The last week had seemed more like a month. Perhaps longer.

"And what makes you believe that she's even alive still?"

"She was taken by a demon. From what we understand, they like to keep their people alive for as long as they have a use for them. We had hoped to be able to track down where she was taken to and rescue her without getting you guys involved."

"And why is that?"

"Because you don't have anyone who specializes in demons," David explained, his frustration making his words sharper than he had intended. He took a calming breath before continuing. "As soon as she was taken, that was the first thing I looked into but if you don't have anyone that can deal with what we have, there isn't a lot that you're going to be able to do to help."

"What makes you so sure that she was taken by a demon?" Charlie asked.

David switched his monitor over to the security system and turned it so that Charlie could see. "Because that's the demon that took her."

Charlie watched the video for a long moment in silence, his brows furled in thought, before nodding quietly to himself. "I guess I need to go speak with your demon, then."

"You can't do that," David pointed out. When Charlie raised a questioning eyebrow, he explained. "She has some sort of mental trick that she plays on any man that gets close to her, it forces them to do what she wants." He turned the monitor back and switched off the video. "So I can't let you go down there."

David explained to Charlie exactly what had happened to Jen, including that it was her own team and close friends who had turned her over and that the demon had in turn handed Jen over, presumably to another demon. "So even though we know where she was taken from and who took her, we don't know where she went from there."

Chapter 2

After being thrown out of the New World office, Troy spent some time pondering his options of what to do next. All of his hubris aside, he was still determined to maneuver himself into the same room as the demoness, if only for a few minutes, but Theo was thwarting him a lot more successfully than he had expected. For a police officer, and a rookie at that, the girl had some talent. He headed down the sidewalk towards his car and groaned as he discovered a parking ticket under his windshield wiper.

He yanked the paper off his windshield and looked around for a trash can but then he had a better idea. He turned around and headed for New World's employee parking garage. Inside, he walked past a number of familiar vehicles.

He recognized Mike's large brown SUV, J.J.'s motorcycle and the little green car with the flower stickers across the back window that belonged to Kelly, the receptionist. When he got to the oversized black pickup that was only in the garage when Theo was there, he lifted the windshield wiper and set the parking ticket underneath. Let her figure it out, he chuckled to himself as he walked back out to the street.

Accepting that he had been thwarted yet again, at least for the day, he headed down to his favorite sandwich shop for some comfort food on a bun. As he waited for his turn to order, he thought back on how they had gotten into this situation. He and Jen had done this type of mission before and they had done a good job every other time. They had tracked things down, he told himself, things that were far more hidden, and they had made things right.

"This wasn't supposed to happen this way," he silently told himself. They were supposed to go in and throw a beat down on the bad guys and then come home and have tacos and beer afterward. Bad things like this were supposed to happen to other people. That's why he was there: to protect her. It had been his only job and he had failed.

His thoughts were interrupted as his turn in line came. He placed his order and went to find a table before letting his thoughts run wild again.

The way he figured it, the night at the demon's house should have gone like clock-work. They went in, exactly as they had planned, more or less, and all they had needed to do was to find the stupid Soul Gem to give back to William, the vampire that had started the whole mess. He was the one that had asked Jen for help and anyone who knew Jen knew that there was no way she could turn down a person in need.

It should have been easy but then somehow everything went wrong. He had been there to protect her; Joel had been there as an added safeguard against the demon as well but, in-stead of keeping her safe, they had ended up being instrumental in Jen's capture. If it hadn't been for them, Jen might still be free.

Now, things were completely sideways and

upside-down. It was like being in a bad dream but he couldn't figure out how to wake up.

Troy slowly smiled as his food arrived. "Exactly like a bad dream and we just need to wake up. That's how we found our targets before," he reminded himself as an idea grew in his head. "I've got to go find the dreamwalker."

He inhaled his food and he knew that if Jen had been there, she would have made a crack that he had wolfed it down. That was one of the things that he liked most about her; she wasn't intimidated by much of anything. Vampires, werewolves, even poltergeists didn't faze her. He just hoped that, wherever she was, she was scaring the crap out of the Derathic dorks that were holding her and that she was giving them enough grief to last a few lifetimes. He wouldn't be surprised if they gave her back, eager to get rid of her.

He knew that it was a false hope but it was a nice thought. Either way, he had a plan.

The dreamwalker, whose real name was Steve Jenkins, was a friend of Jen's and the reason that Troy had started watching over her in the first place. When they had first met the dreamwalker, he had been held captive by a demon that had taken control of his body. With the help of Troy, Jen's brother Patrick, and her team, Jen had been able to free him and destroy the demon's portal so that the demon couldn't come back to this world.

The reason that Troy needed to see the dreamwalker now was because he was probably the only person that could find Jen, if for no other reason than because he had done it many times before. Troy had only learned what his real name was a short time before Jen had been taken, when he overheard her and J.J. talking about a trip they had made to see him. Until then, he had only been known by his title.

Dreamwalkers were a specific breed of psychic that could travel in a dream state to meet with other people who were asleep as well. Because of this, it didn't matter where a person was; if a dreamwalker was looking for them, it was only a matter of time before they fell asleep. If Troy could manage to speak to Steve Jenkins, they could conceivably find her that night.

The last place that Troy knew of that Steve had been was in North Bank Hospital, where he was being held in the long-term care wing. After his bout of being possessed by the demon, the dreamwalker had apparently needed some recovery time. Normally patients wouldn't be accessible to the general public without a damn good reason but Troy had a way to bypass that. Joel worked at North Bank, after all. All he needed to do was ask him to help.

Before getting too deep into his planning, however, he thought better of the idea. If he asked Joel to break the rules for him, Joel might get fired and that would be bad. Although he knew that Joel would be more than happy to put his job on the line if it meant saving Jen, Troy couldn't let his friend risk it. He needed to come up with something else.

On the way, he started to plan for what he would do if he wasn't allowed to see the dreamwalker. In that case, he decided that he would go to the gift shop, get a huge bouquet of flowers and pretend to be from a delivery service. When he got to the hospital, he parked and headed inside to see what he could find.

When he got to the wing where Steve was supposed to be, the nurse on duty shook her head. "Mr. Jenkins is still in his coma," she explained, "and the doctors have ordered no visitors."

Thwarted yet again, Troy walked away. He knew that his initial backup plan of delivering flowers wouldn't work, so now he needed to come up with another one. He paced in the main corridor of the hospital, racking his brain for a way to get into Steve's room but coming up with nothing. He circled around to the backside of the ward he wanted access to and found a set of security doors that looked like they would go to the right place.

Since the doors were locked, he waited in the hallway, trying to look as inconspicuous as possible, until someone opened the doors. He caught one of the doors before it closed and quickly stepped through. The hallway that lay beyond was fairly empty, only the person he had followed and a janitor were visible. Troy knew that he still looked out of place in his street clothes but he didn't see anywhere handy to snatch a set of scrubs to disguise himself as an employee. Instead, he decided that he would just have to be quick about his business.

He didn't know which room Steve was in, so he peeked in through every window he came across and checked the medical files that were neatly placed into holders on the back of the patients' doors. Most of the rooms were empty but a few of them held people that were either badly injured and in need of intensive treatment or who had been in an unchanging state long enough that there wasn't much hope of improvement. The stench of death held in the air, covered by lemon-scented cleaner that hurt Troy's sensitive nose but present nonetheless.

Before he got to the end of the hall, the doors behind him burst open and he heard someone call out, "There he is!"

He turned to look behind him, where he discovered three members of the hospital's security team. Since North Bank was a level 4 hospital, it received all of the high-risk and dangerous patients in the area so their security team was by necessity top notch. The guys heading towards Troy were no exception. All of them were taller than the hybrid and Troy briefly wondered if possessing a visible neck was an automatic exclusion from their company's hiring process.

Two of the officers grabbed Troy, one on each arm, and they bodily lifted him and carried him towards the door. As they escorted him out, the third security officer explained to Troy, "We caught you trying to sneak in on the security cameras. This is a restricted area, so we are going to have to ask you to leave."

"I don't see how I have much of a choice," Troy responded. "You're carrying me."

They brought him all the way to the exterior doors and dropped him on the sidewalk outside. "Don't try anything," the one that had spoken earlier told him. "We'll be keeping an eye out for you."

There was no way that Troy was going to be able to sneak past guards that were on alert, so he headed back for his car. On the way, his phone rang, with a number he didn't recognize.

"Very funny, you dumb Shih Tzu." Theo didn't sound amused. "I'm not paying your barking ticket."

Troy couldn't help but snicker. "Wow, you must have had help with that one."

"Why do you say that? I'm not dumb, you know."

Troy shrugged, even though she wouldn't be able to see it over the phone. "It just seemed to be a bit too polished for a spur of the moment remark."

"It's not. I came up with that one after your stunt in the basement earlier."

"Okay, fine," Troy relented. "I wasn't trying to pick a fight; I was just making an observation." He laughed again as she hung up on him, wondering if she was going to retaliate. Part of him hoped she would and he wondered what she would come up with. Another part of him realized that he really shouldn't be antagonizing her because he knew that it was only happening because he missed his daily bantering with Jen. Again, he wished that Jen was there; she would probably get along famously with Theo.

With no way that he could see to get in and see the dreamwalker, he headed home. He didn't have a place of his own but had instead been living at Jen's house, along with her brother, Patrick. It had seemed to be a good arrangement for the most part. He was there when she needed someone to watch her back and he didn't have to go out and rent an apartment that he wouldn't ever be at. Patrick was there because his construction company had a site in town that he was in charge of and Jen had offered to let him stay at her house instead of renting a place for only a couple of months.

She had seemed to enjoy having them both there but her house had fallen into some publicity recently that she hadn't liked and she had purchased a new house shortly before she was taken. With her gone, Troy and Patrick had been doing most of the packing and getting everything ready to move and Jen's twin brother Todd and their two sisters Jaime and Mary had stayed in town to help as well.

The entire family was home when Troy showed up and he had to park down the block because of the sheer number of vehicles that were already parked in front of the house. Normally Troy wouldn't mind having to walk a little further to get inside but the rain had picked up from that morning and he was cold. As he stepped down the street toward the house, he could almost hear Jen accusing him of smelling like wet dog and he smiled at the thought, even as his gut wrenched with worry.

Soon, he looked toward the sky and promised the rain as it fell, he would bring her home so she could tease him again.

When he walked into the house, the family was in the living room. Jaime, Mary, and Todd were on the couch that Patrick had brought in to replace the one that had been destroyed in a fire not long ago and Patrick was in Troy's recliner.

Jaime was quite possibly the most beautiful woman that Troy had ever seen. It seemed to him that somebody had taken all of the best-looking cover models and rolled them into one gorgeous brunette. He could spend hours looking over the curves of her face and body but the fact that she was friendly and approachable was the whipped cream and cherry on top of an already incredible dessert.

Mary was younger than all the rest. While she wasn't quite as stunning of a beauty as Jaime, Troy could definitely tell that the same foundation was there, wrapped up into the girl next door. Her curly hair was pulled back from her face in a headband but a few locks of hair had escaped to lie against her cheek. What surprised Troy the most about Mary was that her eyes actually sparkled, something that he had always heard people say but this was the first time he'd actually seen it in person. It was just too bad that she had a girlfriend.

It was obvious that Todd was from the same family, even if Troy hadn't known that he was Jen's twin brother. To him, Todd looked like he had just stepped off the cover of a boy-band album, with a little more maturity in his eyes than most would expect from the average teenybopper. He didn't have nearly Patrick's musculature and Troy figured him to be a jogger.

Finally there was Patrick, the red-haired oddity of the family. Troy hadn't ever asked but he figured that there had been a little something on the side as far as Patrick's origins were concerned. Besides the red hair, Patrick was taller and wider than the rest and really looked like the construction worker that he was. He had a scattering of freckles across his face, which would have driven Troy crazy if he'd been cursed with them but for some reason, the ladies seemed to think they were adorable.

For the first little while after Jen had been taken, Patrick had been just short of hostile towards Troy. Jen hadn't let Patrick go with the team when she had gone to the demon's lair but Troy had been included. Since Troy had been supposed to guard Jen, Patrick had laid part of the fault of her kidnapping squarely on Troy's shoulders.

Troy couldn't fault his logic and, to be honest, he had been glad that Patrick hadn't been there. He couldn't imagine how much worse it would have been for Patrick had he been forced to hand his sister over to the demons. However, Patrick's wrath had dimmed significantly and he and Troy, not to mention the rest of the family, had been able to continue working on a plan to find Jen and bring her home. After all, despite their differences, they all shared the same goal.

Todd, a highly trained mage, had set up a work station in Jen's bedroom. This was partly because he could have access to her things, which he had said would help his magic be able to find her, and partly to be away from everyone else where he could have enough peace and quiet to work. He had been locked away in the room, hard at work for the past number of days but from the expression on his face, Troy had the feeling that he hadn't managed to find much.

"I tried all of the location spells I know," he was explaining to the rest of the group as Troy walked to the kitchen to grab a beer. "Nothing seems to be working."

"I thought you had a scrying ball that you used to keep tabs on her," Jaime pointed out. "Isn't that working?"

Todd shook his head. "It just stays blank. That's why I went to my other spells; I thought there might have been a block of some sort over her. But even the most powerful stuff I've got keeps coming up with nothing."

"So... what does that mean?" asked Mary.

"It means that whatever's blocking her is more powerful than I am," Todd regretfully answered. "Either that, or she just plain isn't here."

"Not here?" Jaime asked. "What does that mean?"

Todd shrugged, halfheartedly. "It could mean one of two things. First, she's just not on this plane anymore. That's the theory I'm going with."

"And what's the second theory?" Patrick asked.

Todd hesitated for a long moment before answering. "It could mean not here as in not anywhere. At least if she's on another plane, she's still alive, so that's what I'm looking at."

Troy shook his head at that. "She's still alive, wherever she is." He took a swig of his beer and looked around the group. "The demon bitch tried to kill her at first but then she handed her off to one of her cronies. I'm not sure what that was about but I'm pretty sure it wasn't so that she could be killed somewhere else."

Patrick looked like he wanted to say something about that. Troy waited for it but whatever his comment was going to be was interrupted by a knock at the door.

Since she was the closest to the front door, Mary got up to open it. Everyone else turned to see who it was.

A tall man with short brown hair and brown

eyes stood on the doorstep. He was clean shaven and dressed in a grey suit with a blue tie and expensive shoes. "I'm looking for Troy Franklin, is he available?"

Mary looked over her shoulder at Troy. "It's for you."

Troy stepped forward and set his barely-touched beer down on the coffee table. "I'm Troy."

The man offered his hand. "I'm Charlie Winters. David Melrose told me I could find you here."

Troy took the hand and shook it. "What's this about?"

"It's about Jen Rice. May I come in?"

Taken aback by Charlie's candor, Troy stepped aside so that he could enter. "What do you want to know?"

"According to David, you were with the team when she disappeared, is that correct?"

Suspicious, Troy slowly nodded. "Yes, I was." He reached down and picked up his beer for another drink. This wouldn't be the first time that he had been accused of something simply because he was a hybrid; it was one of the reasons he had been discharged from the military. "What does that have to do with you?" He swirled the amber liquid in the bottle, sure he would need another by the time this conversation was over.

Charlie reached into a pocket inside his jacket and offered him a business card. "I'm with the National Paranormal Investigative Board. We only became aware of Ms. Rice's status as a missing person earlier today."

Troy took the card and looked at it. "What's a staff analyst want with her?"

"I just happened to be the one here when we found out she was missing. Normally, one of our investigation teams would have been sent out but Director Melrose wanted this kept quiet." He looked around at the rest of the group, who were watching the exchange with interest. "If this is a bad time, I can come back later. I hadn't meant to intrude."

Troy shook his head. "No, they've been here since she's been gone." He looked up at Charlie. "Since before that, actually. These are Jen's brothers and sisters."

"I believe I read something about her being

from a large family." He looked at the group more closely. "Would one of you be Patrick, then?"

Troy spoke up before anyone could respond. "Patrick wasn't there when she was taken. He isn't a part of anything."

"I am aware of that and I ask for two reasons. First, Patrick is the only one of you I have a name for." He looked around the group again, his eyes lingering on Todd and Patrick, the only other men in the room. "And second, I understand he accompanied both you and Jen on previous assignments." He looked back at Troy as he finished. "I can understand that you don't want any more people to get involved than you have to but I will need to speak with everyone at some point."

Troy was about to argue further when Patrick stood up. "Its fine, Troy." He looked over at Charlie. "I'm Patrick."

Charlie turned to him and offered a hand. "I am very sorry about the circumstances but I want you to know that I am here to help find your sister." He looked down at Todd at that point. "I don't suppose that you're Joel Peters, are you?"

Todd shook his head and stood up. "My name's Todd."

"I figured it was a long shot but it didn't hurt to ask." He turned back to Troy. "First, I would like a recounting of what happened the night she was taken." He held up a hand before Troy could protest. "I've read the reports, so I know basically what happened, plus I spoke with a couple of the other men she works with for a better picture. But I've learned through experience that there are details that get left out of the reports, not necessarily on purpose, that might hold vital information." He turned to Patrick then. "And I'd like a bit more information about the assignments that you went out on as well, for the same reason."

Patrick looked confused. "Those other things I went out on didn't have anything to do with what happened this time."

"For right now, we're not treating them as connected but this will also give us extra information about Jen herself. How she responds in a stressful situation, thought and behavior patterns, and other things like that. We don't have a preliminary report on her as we would like to have, so the best we can do is reconstruct from other peoples' observations."

He included the rest of her gathered family in his glance. "If you don't mind, I'd like to talk with all of you as well, for the same reason. Families generally know things about each other that aren't as apparent to an outside viewpoint."

"I don't get it," Todd spoke up. "How is a stress analysis profile supposed to help find her?"

Charlie looked surprised. "You're familiar with the process, then?"

"I'm a consultant with Viceroy and I've never seen a stress analysis used for something like this." Viceroy was a magical research and support company that regularly worked with the NPIB. "As far as I've seen, those analyses are only good for profiling high-risk targets and pre-employment screening." He shot Charlie a challenging look. "Somehow, I don't think either of those is going to help us get Jen back."

"No, you're right," Charlie admitted. "The

chance of a stress analysis actually helping to find your sister is fairly low. However, what we're hoping for is that the analysis will give us an idea of how well she would be reacting to her situation at this point, whether she would have attempted to communicate, to escape, and how she would have done any of these. So what I'm suggesting is a bit deeper than just a standard profile."

Todd still didn't look very convinced but he sat back down. "Ask your questions," he said. "But I still doubt that it will help any."

Charlie's first order of business was to have Troy recap his version of the night that Jen was taken. Troy was a bit hesitant about explaining the whole thing in front of the rest of the group but he understood that they already knew most of it and they deserved to hear the whole story. He explained how foggy a lot of his memories of that night were and that the only person that had control over what they were doing had been Jen. "I'm pretty sure that's why the demon wanted her," he said.

Once he had the story from Troy, Charlie turned to Patrick and had him explain about what he had seen, heard, and done while he was assisting the New World team. Patrick explained about the dreamwalker that had been under the control of a different demon, then he explained about the caves beneath the city that he had joined Jen and her team explore to confront the demon. He explained about fighting off the demon and having to go back to the same town again the next day to destroy the demon's gate to Derathim, the plane of dark energy.

"And all that time, nobody even knew that Jen was facing down the possibility of being turned into a werewolf." He explained about the assassin that had tried to kill her while she was in the hospital, waiting to see if she would shift after a werewolf attack, and how Joel had managed to keep the would-be killer from getting to her.

Jaime, Mary, and Todd didn't have much to add to the story. They explained about some of the things they had done as kids and how crushed Jen had been when Todd had developed magical talent but she hadn't. "She became really self-sufficient after that," Jaime explained. "It was the first time that she and Todd had ever been separated, so I guess she felt like she was on her own without him."

"So you two were close, then?" Charlie looked over at Todd.

"We're twins," he answered. "It doesn't get much closer than that."

When he ran out of questions to ask about their family dynamics, Charlie asked about Joel. "He was mentioned in a lot of the New World reports and you guys have mentioned him a few times, too."

Troy shook his head. "He doesn't need to be in the middle of all this."

Charlie sighed. "I know you're just trying to be protective but I really do need to speak with him. He already is in the middle of this but for now it's just a question of getting his side of the story and see if there are any details that he remembers that you might not have caught."

"Not a chance," Troy responded hotly, muscles flexing beneath his still-damp shirt. "That bitch damn near made him kill one of his best friends, then she made us turn her over to that other demon. Joel hasn't been in a very good mood lately and for you to go out there and make him go through it all again will likely just result in your getting hurt." He could feel the hair start to stand up on the back of his neck as his ire rose.

"You think he'd be violent?" Charlie made a note in his notebook.

"He's a hybrid." Troy smirked at him. "And if you know anything about hybrids, you'd know that we can be kind of dangerous when we get backed into a corner."

Charlie pulled out another business card. "Could you at least ask him to give me a call?" When Troy took the card, he nodded. "I know that you guys don't have any reason to trust me right now. Hell, I'd say you have a lot of reasons to not trust anybody. I just want you to know that, even if I am coming in late in the game, I'm on your side.

"Besides that, the NPIB has a lot more resources available than just a scattered group of people. As good as your intentions are, there are bound to be things that you can't do on your own."

Troy thought about it for a moment, looking

down at Charlie's business card as he considered. "You really want to help?" he asked finally. When Charlie nodded, he said, "Do you think you can get Jen's phone records? Not for the house phone, I don't need that, but for her cell phone."

"I probably could," Charlie admitted. "What do you need those for?"

"Because that's the number that the vampire always called her on. If I can get his number, we might have a link to finding where she is." He looked over at Patrick, who nodded approvingly. "Besides, that bastard got her into this mess; none of us would have been there if it hadn't been for him. The way I see it, he owes her. The least he can do is help us look for her."

Charlie pulled his handheld computer from a pocket. He clicked on it for a moment before asking, "What is her number?"

Troy rattled it off, and it was only a few moments before the requested information was downloading. "Where do you want this sent to?" Charlie asked.

Troy gave him the routing number to Jen's house computer. "That way, we all have access to it," he explained to Patrick. He looked back towards Charlie. "I'll let Joel know you want to talk to him. If he feels up to it, he'll give you a call later."

Without more to add, and with the group obviously not wanting to talk further, Charlie left.

Once he was gone, Troy looked around the group. "We need to hurry."

"There's going to be more of them here soon and if we don't find her quickly, we're going to be left completely out in the cold."

"So what do we do?" Jaime asked.

Troy sat at the computer, started printing out the list that Charlie had sent him, and pulled out his phone. "I'm going to call every number in her call log until I find William." He looked over the group as he explained, "He's the vampire that got her into this mess."

Patrick walked over next to him. "I'll help you with that. Two of us will be able to clear more of these numbers than just one."

They started with the first two numbers on the list and each of them marked the one that they were calling, just to be sure that they wouldn't both end up calling the same numbers. "Just worry about the incoming calls," Troy pointed out. "I'm not sure that she ever called him but I know he called her."

"And we can just cross off the numbers that we know who they belong to," Patrick added. "Like this one here, it's mine, and I think that one's to the office, isn't it?"

Troy looked over at the number he was pointing at. He scrolled through his own numbers in his cell phone. "No, that one's Marc's number." He scanned further down the list and pointed to a different line. "That one's the office."

Once they had all the familiar numbers marked off, they started dialing all of the numbers that remained. Most of the incoming calls had been from Sahara Peters, Jen's best friend. They hadn't recognized the number because Sahara had called from her herbal shop, Sugar and Spice.

A couple of calls had been from reporters, which made Troy wince as he realized that these were the people who had driven her from her home. There was a call from the hospital, where she'd had blood tests run a short time ago. Finally, Patrick signaled over to Troy that he had something.

"Is this William?" he asked. "My name is Patrick, and I'm calling you because I'm Jen Rice's brother."

"No, Jen's not okay. She's missing; she went missing while she was investigating your daughter's disappearance." Another long pause. "We were hoping that we could meet with you, to see if there is any information that you could give us that might help find her."

"Yes, I realize that you can't go out in the daytime. We're willing to wait until after sunset. Tomorrow night? That would be perfect. Where would you like to meet?"

"Okay, we'll see you there." When he hung up the phone, everyone was watching. "This is our guy," he explained as he circled the number in red ink. "And he's willing to meet with us."

"So who was this guy again?" Mary asked. "I thought he was just someone that asked Jen to look for his daughter."

"He is," Troy agreed. "But there are two reasons I want to talk to him. First, his daughter was taken by the same demons that took Jen so he might have more information about that. Second, he's the only person besides Jen that I know the dreamwalker has contacted."

"Who's the dreamwalker?" Jaime asked. "Patrick mentioned him when that other guy was here asking questions but I don't think I ever heard of him before."

"His real name is Steve Jenkins and he's a type of psychic who can contact other people in their sleep. He's contacted Jen before, so with any luck, he can contact her again."

Everyone brightened at that idea. "So why don't we just ask this psychic ourselves? Why do we have to get this vampire guy involved?"

"Because Jenkins is still in a coma. I was at the hospital earlier and nobody's allowed in to see him." Troy explained about being thrown out of the hospital by the security staff. "Since I can't sneak back in to see him, this is the only way we have left to contact him."

"If he's in a coma," Mary asked, "then how can William speak to him? Doesn't that mean he can't talk to anyone?"

"Physically, no. But he contacted William

while he was in a coma and I know that Jen spoke with him, too. So it's possible."

With a possible means of communication with Jen on the horizon, everyone's mood brightened considerably. Even if this meant that all they could do was talk to someone who had spoken to her, it was better than the nothing they were all dealing with. Some news was better than no news and there was always the possibility that the dreamwalker could give them vital information towards bringing her home.

However, there wasn't much that they could do with that until their meeting with William the next night. Troy went over to his pack to check his supplies, deciding that the best way he could fill the empty hours was by creating more explosives. The simple act of mixing the components and filling the tubes was calming to the hybrid and the repetitive motion allowed him to clear his mind while doing something productive.

Just after he got started, he received a call from Joel, his best friend. Troy and Joel had grown up together and, since they were both hybrids, they stuck together out of a sense of self-preservation in a mostly human town. "Hey, what's up?"

"I was planning to head up to Cathy's house to do some work on my axes. They keep getting stuck in everything and it's a bit annoying. Cathy offered to let me use her shop because she has the equipment to fix it. You want to come up with?" Joel had been out on a couple of responses with Jen and her team and since he wasn't equipped the way the response team was, Troy had taken over getting Joel geared up. One of the things that Troy had given Joel was a pair of hand axes, good for close combat and to let him use his half-werewolf strength. Joel had put those axes to good use but had apparently damaged one in the process.

"Yeah, I'll go," Troy answered. "I was just making some more bombs but I can wait on that."

"Bring them with you,' Joel suggested. "Cathy has a huge shop out on the back of her property, so it'll be okay to make them there."

"I can do that," Troy agreed. "Are you going

to swing by and pick me up? I don't know where she lives."

Joel agreed, so Troy started to pack down his chemicals and components for transportation. When Joel arrived, he helped Troy carry all of his equipment out to the old blue minivan. Before they left, however, he turned to Joel. "You said you were going to be working on your axes, right?" When Joel nodded, he asked, "Could we work on a new machete for me, while we're at it? Mine got busted a while ago."

"Yeah, no problem."

Troy jogged over to his car and pulled a chunk of steel out of his trunk. He carried the steel over to the minivan and stuffed it into the back along with the rest of his supplies, and the two men headed out of town towards Cathy's house.

Cathy Hartley lived a decent distance outside of town, close enough for her to get to and from work and her daughter to go to school but far enough out so that their closest neighbors were out of eyesight from their house. A single-story house with a rear deck that was almost as large as the rest of the structure took up most of the lot, with an aboveground swimming pool, covered to keep the falling leaves out of it, occupying most of the side yard. A small shop sat at the end of the driveway, at the back corner of the property.

Although Troy hadn't met Cathy previously, he had seen her on a couple of occasions when Jen had brought him to events within her group of friends. She was a tall woman, the three-inch heels on her boots made her even taller than Troy, with unnaturally bright red hair that curled down around her shoulders like a gentle waterfall. Rows of jewelry lined both ears and a smattering of tattoos speckled her arms and one calf.

Although Joel had made it sound as though Cathy would be helping the men as they worked on their assorted weapons, she mostly focused on her own projects, creating molds for resin casting. She only came over to join them when she was needed to hold things in place or to give an opinion.

Among the three of them, they were able to fix Joel's axes, remake Troy's machete, and make a sizeable quantity of explosives. They called it a night just before midnight and loaded all of their stuff back into Joel's van. "Do you think that's going to be enough?" Cathy asked about the explosives as she helped them load.

Troy shrugged. "I'm going to go to the office in the morning to make more rounds for the firearms. I've got a design that I've been working on that will kill pretty much anything, so no matter what gets thrown at us we'll be fine." He grinned, intentionally showing far more fang than he needed to. "By the time I'm done, we'll be able to blow a hole into Derathim and go get her back the hard way, if that's what it comes to."

Cathy nodded approvingly. "Best of luck, then. If you need anything else, let me know."

"We'll do that." Troy stepped up into the van. "Thanks for helping us out with this."

Cathy shook her head. "I may not have been as close to Jen as a lot of you guys were but nobody deserves to be stuck where she's at. So if there's anything I can do, I want you to tell me."

"Thanks," said Troy as Joel started the van. "I'll keep that in mind."

"Is there something going on there that I

should know about?" Troy asked as they pulled away. "I mean, no judgement here, she's gorgeous, but what about your wife?"

"Everything's fine," Joel reassured him. "Cathy and her husband got divorced a couple years ago, so every now and again I come up to check on her and make sure she's okay, do a little maintenance on the house so its not falling all around her, stuff like that. In return, I get to use her shop whenever I want."

Troy spent the entire next day in the New World office basement, locked away in the workroom that David had allotted for him. Since Troy specialized in making unique weapons and ammunition, he had agreed to let the response team use some of his ammunition and explosives in exchange for use of the concrete-reinforced room to build everything in.

He made case after case of explosive rounds, garlic-infused anti-vampire rounds, silver nitrate anti-werewolf rounds, and even more rounds that encompassed everything. Troy liked his anti-everything rounds because with them it didn't matter what you were up against, it wouldn't survive.

At dinnertime, he went upstairs to talk with David. On the way, he ran into Theo, who stopped to glare at him. Troy smiled innocently at her. "I'm on the clock, so you can't throw me out again."

She narrowed her eyes as he turned and walked down the hall towards David's office. He could swear that he could feel her glare burning into his back as he tapped on the director's door, which only served to make his smile even wider.

At David's call to enter, Troy stepped inside. "Hey, boss man, I've got some news and some equipment. You interested in either?"

"What've you got?"

"Well, I'm working on a couple cases of mixed-filling rounds, should be good to use on everything. It's a mix I've used before and they work great." He stopped to think for a moment. "Except spirits," he amended. "They probably wouldn't work too well on spirits."

David chuckled. "If you'd come up with an anti-ghost round, I'd definitely be interested. What's your news?"

Troy grinned and sat in one of the guest

seats in front of David's desk. "We found the vampire."

David's eyes widened. "Really? How did that happen?"

"Your NPIB dude came by and offered to help us find Jen. Kinda useless, really, but he was able to pull out her phone records and we got the Vamp's number from there."

"Excellent." He leaned forward over his desk. "Did he have anything useful?"

"I don't know yet. Patrick and I are meeting him after sundown tonight." He looked around the office. "Hm. I'd figured this place'd be swarming with NPIB agents by now."

David sighed and shook his head. "Their investigation team should be here in a few days, so whatever you're going to do, do it quickly. I can't control what will happen once they get here."

"I know," Troy agreed. "Those guys just swarm in and take over everything. The worst part, even if they do manage to find Jen, we wouldn't get her back."

"Why do you think that?"

"Because she's been to the other side. At

the very least, they'd want to keep her under observation."

David couldn't fault his logic. "I don't know much about what they'd do with her once they found her but I still think it'd be best if we kept doing what we can. Keep me informed of what you find and if you need anything, let me know and I'll do what I can to get it for you."

"What if I said I needed a date with Theo? Could you get that for me?"

David laughed for the first time in days. "I doubt that even God himself could get that for you."

"Damn," Troy swore. "Ah, well. It was worth a try." He stood up and headed for the door. "There's a couple of cases of ammo downstairs for your guys. I'll let you know what happens with the Vamp." As he opened the door, he looked back at David. "Did you know that the dreamwalker is still in a coma?" When David nodded, Troy explained, "The doctors aren't allowing any guests but I had thought Jen had been allowed in to see him a while ago."

"She was but it was by special request. If I'd known you were going there, I would have told you not to bother. He still isn't communicating."

"Well, I'm going to see what I can do to fix that." He checked his watch. "But I have to go. I'm supposed to be in a meeting in half an hour."

Chapter 3

Patrick sat in the coffee shop where William the vampire had agreed to meet him. He had expected Troy to be there as well but the hybrid had been busier than usual lately. He drummed his fingers on the table and took another sip of his latte. Although he wasn't normally as much of a coffee drinker as his little sister was, he figured that the extra caffeine boost wouldn't hurt, all things considered. He had been burning the candle at both ends for a while now and it was starting to wear him down.

While he waited, he looked around. There weren't very many people in the shop, mostly just a bunch of kids from the local college who were apparently working on some sort of a group project. There were a handful of desserts in a glass cage a few feet away from him and he eyed, not for the first time, a frosted muffin that was prominently displayed. He had been debating over the sweet treat for the last ten minutes that he had been waiting at his table and temptation finally won.

He stood up and walked over to the counter to ask for the muffin. When he turned back to his table, he discovered another man sitting in one of the previously vacant seats across from where he had been sitting only moments before. The newcomer was fairly short with brown hair and eyes and was dressed in blue jeans and a waist-length black leather coat. Hoping that this was William and not just someone that had decided to take his table, Patrick walked over and sat down. "I sure hope you're William," he said.

The other man nodded and answered in a clipped British accent, "I am, and I assume that you are Patrick." He looked around the coffee shop. "I am surprised; I had expected to see at least Troy here with you."

"He was supposed to be here; I'm not sure where he is."

"Perhaps caught in the traffic," William offered "It's worse than usual right now." He smiled over at Patrick without revealing any hint of fang. "I believe on the phone you had mentioned that Jen was in some sort of trouble?"

"Yeah, you could say that." Patrick took a bite of his muffin, which didn't taste anywhere near as good as it had looked. "The demon that has your daughter, she took Jen now too." He set the pastry down onto the table, not sure of whether he would finish it off or not. It had to be healthy, he decided. That was the only way it could look that good and still taste that bad. Or maybe it was just the topic of conversation that had dulled its flavor. Whichever it was, he didn't particularly care.

William's eyes widened at Patrick's statement. "I had no idea," he stammered. "May I ask what happened?"

Patrick explained the basics of what had happened but chose to leave out the details. William was obviously shaken by the news and Patrick figured that he didn't need to know exactly how bad it had been for Jen. "So you understand why we want to know everything you know about these demons."

"I understand but I'm afraid I won't be of much use. I never spent much time with the demoness; all I did was retrieve the items she told me to and hand them over to her once I had them. I've never even been to her residence, so I wouldn't know where to direct you."

As Patrick thought about this, the door to the coffee shop swung open and Troy stomped inside, shaking water off his coat. Spotting the pair at the table, he headed directly for them, detouring briefly to order a coffee. "Sorry I'm late," he apologized as he sat down. "There was an accident on the highway. Some idiot hydroplaned and slammed another car into the rails." He looked over at William. "Have we gotten very far yet?"

William shook his head. "Patrick here was just explaining about what had happened to Jen. I am deeply sorry but I don't know of any other information that might help you."

Patrick looked over at Troy. "You said that you guys hadn't managed to find the Soul Gem, right?"

"After what happened, we weren't exactly focused on that. We were mostly looking for Jen and then we had to get the demoness somewhere safe before she started up with her mind tricks again." As he spoke, he reached over and snagged Patrick's mostly-uneaten muffin. When Patrick made no move to stop him, the hybrid shoved the last of the treat into his mouth.

"That's what I thought." Patrick looked over at William as Troy began making choking sounds and gulping at his steaming paper cup of coffee. Maybe it really was just the muffin after all, he decided with no small amount of pleasure. Would teach the hybrid to steal from other people's plates at the very least. "How about we make a trip out to the demon's house? You can have a look for yourself and see if you can find the Gem and we can take another look around while we're there, just to see if the team overlooked anything."

William thought that was a great idea. "When would you like to go?"

Patrick shrugged. "I don't have anything

scheduled, so we could go tonight, if we wanted to."

Troy agreed, glaring at Patrick. "The sooner, the better, I think." He looked over at William, his expression fading back to normal. "Has anyone from the NPIB gotten in touch with you lately?"

William shook his head. "Was my involvement in the thefts reported already?" The demon holding his daughter's Soul Gem had forced William to commit a number of difficult and highly publicized robberies. The vampire had ceased his thievery as soon as Jen had agreed to help him but everyone knew that he would likely be facing punishment once his involvement in the thefts was revealed.

Patrick shook his head. "No. They're looking for Jen too but we're trying to find her before they do."

"Understandable," William agreed. "Sometimes it's hard to tell which side of the legal line that group is truly on."

As soon as Troy's coffee arrived, he stood up. "Shall we go, then? No point in hanging out and talking about it."

Everyone agreed, so they stood and headed for the door. "Maybe you guys should ride with me," Troy pointed out to Patrick. "I have room in my car for six and I know your truck only holds three. Besides, I know where I'm going."

"I believe that I would rather follow in my car, if it's all the same," William explained. "There are certain items inside that I would prefer not to leave behind."

"That makes sense," Patrick agreed before Troy could argue. Everyone headed out to the parking lot and Troy and Patrick waited in Troy's car for William to be ready before heading out onto the street.

Although he hadn't been out this way before, Patrick had a strange sense of familiarity as they drove. He wondered whether things would have been different if he had been with the group the last time they had been out this way. Even though he knew that if he had been there he would probably have fallen victim to the demoness's charms like everyone else had, there was still a part of him that believed that he wouldn't have, that he could have saved his sister somehow.

He snapped out of his reverie as they turned off the highway. Closer to where Jen had been taken from and to possibly discovering new clues as to where she had gone, he felt the need to pay closer attention to his surroundings. One thing that surprised him was how far outside of town they had travelled. "I thought this was in closer."

Troy shook his head. "Nope, we've still got a little way to go yet."

"How much further?" Patrick wondered if they should have stopped for fuel before getting this far out of town. There was less than a quarter tank of gas registering on the dashboard gauge and Patrick had no doubt that Troy's car would suck down the entire remaining fuel if he put the accelerator to the floor.

"Ten, maybe fifteen minutes before we get there."

Patrick was surprised. The houses and landscaping in the area were beautiful and far more expensive than he had imagined for a demon to be living in. He estimated that most of the houses they were passing were in the million-dollar range, if not higher.

They stopped in front of a large, wrought iron gate at the end of a driveway. The gates were open and one of them sat at an angle as though it had been forcibly opened from within. "This is it," Troy said as he turned off the car. "The house is just a little way up there."

William pulled up and parked his small green sedan behind them. As he stepped out, he whistled low at the sight. "Looks like someone was in a hurry to get out of there."

"Yeah," Troy agreed. "We were." He popped his trunk open and pulled out a large black duffel bag, which he tossed over to Patrick. Confused, Patrick peeked inside the bag, where he discovered the tactical gear that Troy had put together for him the first time Patrick had gone out with the team. When he looked up, Troy was smiling knowingly at him. "Figured that sooner or later you were going to want that."

Patrick pulled on the protective vest. There wasn't any place to get changed into all of the clothes that were packed into the bag but at least he was going to wear the armor. Even though the New World team had cleared the building and found that there was nobody left inside, that had been a week ago and there was no way to know who – or what – had showed up in the meantime. "Are we expecting any-thing to be inside?" he asked as he adjusted the straps.

Troy shrugged. "No way to tell, really. But we know that there's a demon out there that has already gone in and out of this place at least once that we know of. If he's in there some-where, I want to be ready for him." As he spoke, he pulled out his own gear bag and started to get ready.

Patrick pulled the pistol out of its pocket and slipped it into its holster. He adjusted the belt that held the holster and buckled it around his waist. Once he had everything sitting where he wanted it, he looked over at Troy. "Are we ready?"

Troy pulled a pair of shotguns out of his trunk before slamming it shut. He tossed one of them over to Patrick and nodded. "As ready as we're going to get."

Troy and Patrick led the way up the drive-way, with William staying close behind. As they walked, William asked, "Why didn't we just drive up to the house? Wouldn't that have been faster?"

Troy shook his head. "Last time, there were guardians on duty. I don't know if there'll be any here now but I don't want to announce that we're coming, just in case anyone's watching."

"But we're walking directly up the driveway. If we're trying to keep out of sight, wouldn't it make more sense to come in from the side?"

"Not much point in that," Troy explained. "The grounds are pretty flat and there isn't a lot of foliage to hide behind." He looked over his shoulder at the vampire as he spoke. "The only reason I didn't want to drive up to the house was because of the noise. Walking is a lot quieter."

They made it up to the house without being accosted. Troy opened the door and peeked inside, scouting for anyone or anything that could be waiting for them. After a moment, he stood straighter and motioned that it was safe. He opened the door further and stepped through, groping for the light switch as he entered.

Patrick followed him in, eager to see where everything had transpired. He still didn't know all the details of what had happened and where but he did know that it had all started in the entrance hall.

Stained glass windows reflected the lights from the chandelier overhead, casting beams of colorful light across the plush carpet and dusty tapestries that covered the otherwise bare walls. Each window featured a different scene set into the stained glass but they appeared to tell a story with each of them leading into the next. Some of them were landscape scenes but others featured people and animals, all of which seemed to be dancing and celebrating.

Patrick wasn't sure why, but the windows gave him the creeps even more than anything else in the room did.

Beneath each pane of glass, a low wooden table sat. Most of them held small decorative items, such as a bird shaped from bronze, a blue vase with a dead flower in it, and a round mirror with a trio of deep purple candles sitting on it. All of the tables and decorations were covered with a thin layer of dust and a couple of the tables were devoid of decoration entirely.

On their left a long hallway led further into

the house and to their right a heavy wooden door stood slightly ajar. At the end of the room, a large sweeping staircase led up to the next floor. The staircase was made of smooth marble with a wide carpeted runner placed down the center to protect the steps. Patrick looked over at Troy, not sure where to go next.

Troy looked up at the top of the stairs. "The demon bitch was up there when we arrived," he explained in a low voice as he gestured toward the landing. "Just standing at the top of the staircase and watching us." He looked over at Patrick and William, his eyes haunted by the memory. "We were all down here; we stopped just inside the door just like this."

Patrick nodded. "Do you remember where you went from here?"

Troy thought for a moment. "Jen was arguing with her but everything went fuzzy at that point so I don't really remember all of it. I remember that Jen charged towards the stairs, I think to get to the demon. I stopped her but I'm not sure why. Probably the bitch's fault again." He took a couple of halting steps toward the staircase before stopping. "I think the demon came down here while I was holding Jen."

He turned and looked around the room. He took a couple of steps toward the open door before stopping to head the other way. As he walked toward the hallway, he continued to explain. "We followed her, all of us. I think she led us this way. Jen was fighting and yelling the whole time."

He looked back towards the front door where Patrick and William still waited. When he spoke again, his voice was barely more than a whisper. "It was over here. I pulled her with me, and we went this way."

Patrick and William followed the hybrid down the hall and through another solid wooden door. In the next room, there were no more stained-glass windows but the walls were still covered by hanging tapestries. In the center of the room, a large stone table caught Patrick's attention. It was scraped and gouged across most of the surface, dark brown and black stains mottled the stone. Even though there was a faint memory of the demoness ordering Joel to cut out Jen's heart, Troy didn't want to admit what had caused the discoloration. "This is where the rest of it happened?"

"First, she had us put Jen on the table. I think she was going to sacrifice her or something, at least that's what it seemed like, but Jen fought back. When she couldn't kill her, she had us pick her up and hold her over here." He stepped around to the other side of the table.

"Then there was another demon here, a male, but I'm not sure where he came from." His eyes fell to the floor. "We handed her over to him and he disappeared with her." His jaw clenched in anger, as did his fists.

It was almost a full minute before Patrick broke the silence. "If the Gem is here, it's probably in this room, then."

Everyone agreed, so they began to search the room. There wasn't a lot to search besides the stone table and small bookcase against one wall. There were no books on the shelves, only a carved wooden box, a handful of newspapers that seemed oddly out of place, and vials of a thick liquid that appeared to be blood. With one sniff, William was able to verify the vials' contents. "I have no idea how old these are but they're rancid." He set them back onto the shelf and opened the box. Hope was clearly written on his face as he lifted the lid.

That hope quickly faded as he closed the lid again. "It's the dagger I took from the museum," he explained. He sighed and set the box onto the scarred stone table. "I guess this should go back to the museum, though. There's no reason to leave it here."

Troy nodded his agreement. "Maybe you could sneak back in and put it back. That way, it's like it wasn't really stolen, just misplaced."

"That's a terrible idea," Patrick pointed out. "You really think they're going to believe that they just missed it somehow?"

"Besides," William interjected, "they've updated their security system after the break-in. I'm not sure I'd be able to get past it again."

"I know," Troy sighed. "I was just trying to think of a way for you to not end up in the slammer over this."

"If that's what is to happen, I am already at peace with that," William smiled at him. "All that concerns me is that my Rachel is returned to me before I am locked away."

It didn't take long for them to verify that the Soul Gem wasn't anywhere in that room. "I guess we should look through the rest of the house," Patrick pointed out.

"We went through it last time we were here," Troy said, "but we were looking for signs of where Jen may have been taken to. None of us were really focused on looking for the Gem, so it still might be here somewhere."

"Understandable, given the circumstances," William said. "And while we look, we may see something that may lead to Jen as well."

There were no other doors leading out of the space they were in, so they headed back down the hallway and into the entrance area. The first place that they decided to check was beyond the only other door in the room, which only led to another hallway but that corridor had other doors leading off of it. They searched a library, kitchen and dining areas and what seemed to be a laboratory of some sort.

There was a table in the center of the laboratory but this one wasn't made of stone, instead crafted of a sturdy hardwood. There were scales and other measuring devices placed on the table and the counters that lined two walls, as well as a handful of heating plates and cooking utensils. Shelves lined the walls above the countertops, each of which was filled with bottles and jars of colorful liquids and fine powders.

"What the hell is all this?" Patrick wondered as he looked around the room.

"Ecstasy," Troy supplied, looking slightly confused. "There was supposed to be a HazMat team come in here and clean this up a while ago."

"The demon was making drugs?" William asked. "That doesn't make sense."

Troy shrugged. "A lot of things don't make any sense lately." With all of the other craziness that had been cropping up lately, the demon-created drugs barely even registered on his weird-shit-o-meter.

After they finished searching the downstairs, the trio headed up the grand staircase to the next floor. In the upstairs hall, they found more tables lining the hallway, with more bric-a-brac on them. Two of the things that caught Patrick's eye were a bowl of jewels that still shone brightly despite the thin layer of dust that had settled over everything and a silver filigree tiara that he recognized from the news. "Isn't that the Tiara of Venus you stole?" he asked William.

The vampire walked over to pick up the relic. "I'm honestly not sure whether I am confused or relieved. I hadn't expected that she was having me steal things just for decoration." He turned the tiara over in his hands. "But then, I can't think of what this could be used for other than just a lovely trinket." He set the headpiece back down on its pedestal. "Other than the obvious purpose, of course. Certainly it was created to be worn."

Each of the rooms on that floor was a bedroom, a restroom, or a closet. The bedrooms were ornate, with thick blankets and comforters and silk or satin sheets on each of the beds, of which there were plenty. The bathrooms were all fully stocked as well, with plenty of soaps and towels laid out as though the demoness had been expecting guests when the team had arrived.

The last bedroom they arrived at was

different than the rest. For starters, it was the only locked room they had found in the house, so Troy had to pull a set of tools out of his gear belt to pop the lock open.

When he opened the door, everyone stared in shock. Where all of the other rooms were light and airy, with decadent furnishings and plush comfort, this room was stark and utilitarian. The walls were paneled in dark wood, unlike the tapestry-covered and light-colored walls in the rest of the house. The floor was hard wood as well but there was an array of equipment in it that Patrick couldn't imagine what it was used for.

Against one wall, a rough wooden device stood almost seven feet tall. It was X-shaped, with thick leather cuffs on each arm and leg. Next to that, a row of cupboards was attached to the wall. The doors were closed and he wasn't sure he wanted to know what was hiding inside, but he knew that they would end up investigating, regardless of his apprehension.

A bar hung suspended from the center of the ceiling on thick chains, with more leather cuffs attached at each end of the bar and in the center. The metal of the bar was polished to a high shine, contrasting brightly against the black leather.

There was a chair against another wall that almost looked harmless in comparison to everything else in the chamber. It was smooth wood and metal, with a pair of armrests and footpads. Just as with everything else in the room, the chair had leather straps on the armrests and footpads. There was also a control panel attached to the side but from the doorway, Patrick couldn't tell what it was supposed to do.

"What the hell is this place?" he finally managed to ask.

Troy shrugged. "Torture chamber, as far as I can tell." He stepped further into the room. "I wasn't in here before but I remember a couple of the guys talking about it."

"If this room was already searched, how did the door get locked again?" Patrick asked as he followed him over to the row of cabinets.

Troy pulled out his lock picks again. "The guys couldn't look in these before, so I don't even know what's in them."

When he finally opened the first cupboard,

Patrick stepped back in horror. Whips, paddles that looked similar to the ones that came with a ping-pong table, and thick leather straps hung in neatly-organized rows behind the doors. The next cupboard held more of the same, as did the one beyond.

Patrick couldn't stand to stay in that room any longer, so he joined William, who had already retreated out into the hallway. "Pure evil," he explained to the vampire. "That's what they are, just pure evil." He shuddered again as they waited for Troy to join them.

When the hybrid came out, he closed the door behind him. "There wasn't anything that could have been the Gem in there," he explained to them without making eye contact with either of his companions. "There weren't any secret passages or anything like that, either.

"It looks like neither of them is here," William commented sadly as they headed towards the stairs. "But at least we can get these back to their rightful owners." He held up the box that held the dagger, with the tiara balanced on its lid. "That's more than we had when we arrived."

At the bottom the stairs, William and Patrick

headed for the door, but Troy stopped. "That's strange," he muttered, more to himself than to either of them. "I thought there were things on all of the tables." He walked over to one of the wooden tables that had nothing on it and looked around the base. He reached down behind it and pulled up a star-shaped crystal. With a sigh, he placed it back on the table. "I don't know..."

He was interrupted by William, who rushed forward to pick up the crystal. "Rachel," the vampire breathed as he cradled the crystal in his hands.

Troy looked over at the vampire, eyes wide. "That's Rachel?" he asked. When William nodded, he chuckled. "Had I known that, I could have gotten her back to you the first night." He peered more closely at the Gem. "Not what I had expected, I guess."

The Gem was almost two inches across and appeared to be made of millions of strands of spun glass, tightly woven together with thin spikes protruding out at every possible angle. William smiled sadly down at the stone. "Rachel always had a flair for the dramatic. A simple, round Gem simply wasn't her style."

Troy clapped him on the back. "Glad to help." He looked back at Patrick and then at William again. "I hope you still intend to help us find Jen; she did go missing while trying to find your daughter."

"Of course," William reassured him. "Whatever I can do, I am your servant. No matter what you need, you have only to ask."

"Great," Patrick walked up to stand next to them. "There is, actually, something that you can do."

"Anything," William answered.

"We need you to contact the dreamwalker," Patrick explained. "We're pretty sure that he can contact Jen and maybe even tell us where she is so we can get her."

William looked doubtful at that. "I'm not sure how to do that. I never had to contact him, he always approached me."

"I know," Patrick reassured him, "but I think we have a way that can help with that."

"How? I'm not a psychic, so I don't know how to reach out to him."

"Jen had the same problem but a friend of ours is an herbalist who makes a tea that has let Jen get into contact with him when she needed to in the past. That tea should work for you, too."

William was willing to try, so they headed out to the cars. On the way back to town, Patrick called Sahara. "Sorry to call you so late but is there any way you can meet us at Sugar and Spice in about an hour?"

Sahara Peters was Jen's best friend, so it was no surprise that he was able to talk her into meeting them at the shop in the middle of the night. All he had to do was explain that they might have found a way to find Jen and she was wide awake and ready to go.

When they pulled up in front of Sugar and Spice, the herbal shop that Sahara owned, the lights were on inside and they could see some-one moving around. Patrick hopped out as soon as the car stopped rolling and headed for the door. It was locked when they arrived but at his knock, Sahara came up to let them in.

Sahara Peters was in her early thirties, with a riot of multicolored curls that were stuffed under a black beanie cap that had a yellow bat embroidered on the side. She was dressed in fuzzy leopard-printed pants and a short-sleeved shirt that proclaimed she was "Hanging with my Gnomies." She had apparently decided against putting her contacts back in, instead wearing thin silvery-framed glasses. Patrick gave her a quick hug and stepped inside.

"What's going on? Did you really find her?" Sahara asked as she locked the door behind them.

Patrick shook his head. "Not yet but we've got a lead."

"What can I do to help?"

"You remember that dream tea that you made for Jen?" Troy asked. "We need some for William, too."

Sahara's face fell. "That stuff doesn't let you do what she thought it did. All that does is help to get rid of nightmares." She looked over at William and blinked at him a couple times. "Are you a vampire?" He nodded and Sahara sighed. "On top of everything I just said, this tea wasn't designed for vampires. I don't know what'll happen if you take it." She stopped to think for a moment. "Probably just nothing, but I don't know for sure."

"I understand that," he said as she pulled a packet of tea marked *Dreamless* from a shelf and handed it over. "But if it will help to find Jen, it is the least I can do."

Sahara waved off Patrick as he tried to pay. "It's not that expensive but I just want you guys to know that it won't help you contact the dreamwalker. I told Jen that a lot too and I don't understand why she never believed me."

"Because every time she used it, she was able to talk to him," Troy explained. "Even if it was just accidental, you know how Jen is. If she can see it, she'll believe it."

"I know." She opened the door again so that they could leave. "Just let me know if you do find anything, okay?"

The men agreed, so she locked the door behind them.

Chapter 4

Once everyone was gone, Sahara turned off the lights and headed into her office in the back of the shop. She set the alarm and let herself out the back door, where her car, a little red station wagon, was waiting. Despite her assertion that the tea wouldn't work, a secret part of her was hopeful that it would. She knew that it seemed to work for Jen, which was something that she had never understood. She had given the tea to other people to see how they reacted but none of them had experienced anything beyond the deep, restful sleep for which the mixture was intended.

When she pulled into her driveway, she could see Joel's shadow as he paced in the living room. She had told him that Troy and Patrick had come up with something as soon as they had called her, so he was waiting to see if Jen had been found. Sahara wasn't sure how to tell him that their big plan had involved a vampire and her dreamless tea.

Joel had been kicking himself ever since Jen had been taken and Sahara could completely understand why. Not only had he handed one of his best friends over to the demon that still held her captive, he had almost killed her before that. While the rest of Jen's team had held her motionless, the demoness had given Joel a stone dagger and instructed him to remove her heart.

Under the demon's thrall, he had done his best to comply.

Not for the first time, Sahara was thankful that her best friend was a fighter. Not many people could escape a hybrid that was intent on murder. Sahara still wasn't sure how the demoness had been able to capture the minds of so many people at the same time; even the most powerful psychics she had heard of were only able to hold complete control over two, maybe three at a time. She suspected that it had something to do with the fact that it was only men that the demoness was able to control but she couldn't be sure.

Unsurprisingly, her research had revealed only that there wasn't a lot of information to be found on demons, other than various religious texts from cultures around the world. Even so, there had been nothing that Sahara had been able to uncover that shed any light on the mystery. Because of the male dominance, the only clue she had to go on, she thought it may have something to do with pheromones and made a mental note to do more research into those chemicals later. She hadn't done much work with pheromones before but if she could come up with a way for the men around Jen to not be sucked in by the demoness again, or similar tactics in the future, it couldn't hurt to try.

"Hey, honey." Joel walked over to her as soon as she stepped in the door and leaned down to kiss her. Since he was almost a foot taller than she, he had to bend quite a distance to achieve that but ten years of marriage had taught him technique.

"The kids are still in bed," he explained.

"I just checked on them a few minutes ago." Sahara and Joel had three boys: Don, who was eight; Nicholas, who was five; and Collin, who had just celebrated his first birthday. Of the three, only Nicholas had inherited the wolf gene from his father and he was as unmanageable as any other young hybrid. Because of that, he also had a hard time sleeping when the moon entered either it's full or its new phase. Tonight was the second night of the new moon, so he was as restless as ever.

Just to be on the safe side, because Nicholas rarely slept through the night during a lunar event, Sahara went into the kitchen to brew some of the relaxation tea that she kept on hand for precisely these occasions. This was a mild brew by her regular standards but she could make a cup and leave it out for Nicholas who could then drink it and go back to sleep when he woke up during the night. Just in time, she realized as she snuck into her son's bedroom. He was already becoming restless. She quietly set the mug to cool on his nightstand where he could easily find it and retreated back to the living room to rejoin her husband.

She dropped her jacket onto the back of the couch and kicked off her shoes, which she hadn't bothered tying in the first place. "I'm not so sure about their great plan," she explained as she sank onto the cushion. She told Joel about the guys bringing a vampire into the picture and having him use her tea to contact the dreamwalker.

"I thought you said it didn't work like that," Joel commented once she was finished. This wasn't the first time they had discussed Jen's beliefs about the tea, so the discussion was irrelevant. However, Joel knew his wife well enough to recognize that she needed to have hope in something and that if there was any way that her tea could help to bring her friend home safely, she would do whatever it took.

He also recognized how truly worried she was, even if she didn't show the normal outward signs. As often as Jen landed herself into trouble, she had never managed to land in water as near to boiling as this. With virtually nothing that she could do to help, Sahara needed to lean on someone, even if that leaning consisted of nothing more than his being supportive of her midnight run to reopen the store.

"It doesn't," she agreed. "But Jen was convinced it did and apparently that was good enough for them."

"On a Vamp?" Joel asked. "I wouldn't think that'd work on one of those at all."

Sahara shook her head. "I don't think it will either but they were determined to try. So I gave them some." She shrugged. "What's the worst that could happen? It doesn't do anything. But if it does work, by some miracle, we've got something."

"Doesn't hurt to try, does it?"

"Nope," a voice called out from the kitchen. The voice was followed by a ghost, floating a few inches off the ground and yet walking at the same time. It looked like a man in his thirties, long blond hair hanging in a ponytail down his back and slightly balding on top. He had changed his facial hair since the last time Sahara had seen him, now he appeared to be clean-shaven. He wore drab green pants with extra pockets down the sides and a black long-sleeved shirt. "Never hurts to try. Failure might be kind of painful but even that depends on what you're failing at."

"Lewis," Sahara said. "I didn't know you were back in town." She had long ago stopped asking the spirit why he changed his appearance so often, or his incessant need for pockets. As a ghost, he couldn't put anything in the pockets – not that he really needed anything in the first place – but he always seemed to make sure to have plenty on hand. Or on pants, as the case seemed to be lately.

"Yep," the apparition answered. "It's been a while, so I decided to drop in and see what was up."

"He means that literally," Joel explained. "He came in through the ceiling, pretending he was Santa."

Sahara had to snicker at that thought. "A little early for that, isn't it?" she asked.

"Nope," Lewis answered. "Have you seen the stores lately? They've already got Yule stuff up and sales going on." He shook his head. "Crazy."

"I've been telling him about what's been going on since he's been gone," Joel explained to Sahara. "And I think we might have an idea of who the vampire is that Troy and Patrick brought over."

"Yeah?" Sahara accepted the cup of coffee that Lewis offered her. "What's so special about him?"

Lewis settled down on the couch next to her, tucking his bare feet under him as he sat. "Well, I remember hearing about this guy a while ago and if it's the same guy, it'd answer a lot of the questions Joel said everyone still had.

"A long time ago, there was a thief that was damn good. I mean, really good. Guy was an artist when it came to getting past everything. But then he just disappeared for a while. People thought he had gotten killed but then he turned back up, only now he was in a different area.

"Used to be he took expensive stuff, jewels and art, high-dollar things. Now, he started taking magical stuff: books and components. Rumor had it, he even kidnapped a mage once, tried to get him to perform some magic for him. Nobody ever knew what was going on with him but if my timeline's right, and the story Joel was telling me about this Vamp's daughter is accurate, then it could be the same guy."

"But vampires can't have kids, can they?" Sahara asked. "The mother always dies before carrying the baby to term."

"Most of the time, yeah, but there have been cases of a few of them surviving. There's even a clinical disease associated with it; I can't remember what it's called but the kid's born with a blood deficiency and has to have extra blood its whole life. Still human, but constantly sick."

"Do you mean porphyria?" Joel asked.

"Yep, that's it. Terrible disease."

"So you think this Vamp's daughter was one of those?" Sahara asked. "That's awful."

Lewis shrugged. "She might be, or the guy might have had her before he was turned. All of this was before Vamps were legal, so I don't know if he was a Vamp back then or not."

"Explains how he was able to pull off those thefts, then."

"I can probably find out more about him later," Lewis offered, "but right now, we need to focus on Jen. I haven't heard anything but I can definitely keep an ear out."

They talked for a while longer but it was late and Sahara had to be at the shop in the morning so she called it a night before much longer. As she climbed into bed, she sent up a quick prayer that the tea would work after all and that they would bring Jen home safely, and soon.

Because she had been up so late, Sahara was groggier than usual the following morning. She stopped at a drive through coffee stand for a white mocha with coconut, her favorite, and almost burst into tears as she remembered that it was Jen's favorite too. Any time she'd had to wake Jen up early in the morning, coconut white mocha was the only thing that got her friend out of bed. She would do just about any-thing to have a reason to order a second cup from the drive through.

Mornings at Sugar and Spice were normally quiet, that day was no different. Sahara was thankful for that; she had some paperwork that she had been letting slide a bit too long and there were bills due. She brought her paper-work up to the front counter and sat on her favorite stool so she could get some of it ac-complished while still keeping an eye out for potential customers.

Sugar and Spice was one of the most-respected herbal shops in town, some believed on the entire west coast, and Sahara prided herself on keeping it that way. She had won a handful of awards and honorable mentions over the years and even had some residual income from a recipe she had developed years ago. She specialized in werewolf medications and pregnancy and childbirth aides but after Nicholas was born, she had started toying with the idea of expanding to hybrid medications and early childhood treatments. She had a lot of recipes for different ailments that were already well known and established but she wasn't sure if she wanted to stretch her specialty out that far.

Just past noon, one of her regulars walked into the shop. Sahara put her papers down on the counter and smiled over at him. "Hey, Bobby, what's up?"

Bobby was a werewolf who came in at least once a week to get a stomach remedy. For thirty days out of the month he was a vegetarian but on full moons he gorged himself on meat. Since that was the only time he ate any type of meat, his body didn't react well to it and for the rest of the month he was plagued by indigestion. Sahara pulled down a bottle of his usual medication and set it on the counter.

Bobby sighed and looked over his shoulder towards the door he had just walked through. "Have you had a guy called Roam come in here lately?" His expression, usually calm, was bothered as he asked.

She thought for a moment. "Doesn't ring a bell. Is everything okay?"

"No, no it's not." He looked back towards the door again before leaning against the counter near her. "He's this wacko with some sort of paranormal research thing going on. Conspiracies and government cover-ups everywhere; you know the type. He's been popping up all over town, harassing people and asking all kinds of obnoxious questions of everyone."

Sahara blinked at him. "What does this have to do with me?" Sure, there were tons of conspiracy nuts out in the world but so far none of them had given her any reason to be concerned.

Bobby sighed. "I just wanted to warn you

that he's probably going to be in here bothering you pretty soon."

"Why's that?"

"Two reasons. First, you cater to us Weres and that seems to be enough to get his conspiracy feelers out. But the second reason I wanted to mention it is because I'm in here. That pretty much guarantees that he's going to pay you a visit; probably sooner than later."

"Is this a joke?" She wasn't sure whether to laugh or not.

He shook his head and gestured toward the front window of the shop. "Look out there; he's parked across the street."

Doubtful but willing to humor one of her best customers, Sahara stepped around the counter and walked up to the door. She opened it wide, waiting to see if it was one of the notorious pranksters that stopped in to pester her in occasionally, but there was nothing.

She looked further out and discovered that there was someone suspicious out there, after all.

Parked across the street in a dark grey van, a person sat with a pair of binoculars to his eyes and what appeared to be a video recorder pointed towards her. She couldn't see what the driver looked like but there was a pouf of dark hair sticking almost straight up above the binoculars.

Still standing in the doorway, Sahara turned to look back at Bobby. "So why's this guy following you?"

"I got stuck outside for the last lunar event," Bobby explained. "I was heading for the hospital but my car wouldn't start and I shifted in my driveway." He was quick to add, "I didn't hurt anybody. One of my neighbors called it in pretty fast, so there was a response team there before I got to anyone. I got tossed in lockup until I shifted back and this guy's been trying to figure out why I wasn't put down. Apparently the way he figures it, they should have just taken me out instead of taking me in."

The irritation was obvious on his face and Sahara wasn't entirely positive if it was all because of the stranger's questions or Bobby's own inability to get to safety before the moon's power hit him. As he continued to explain, she had her answer.

"He's been following me around since then, bothering everyone I talk to as if he's trying to figure out why I was spared. He's been to see my boss, all of my neighbors; even my wife hasn't been able to avoid him."

"That's awful!" Sahara exclaimed as she looked back across the street. The man had lowered his binoculars so she was able to get a better look at him. He was thin and dark-skinned and was now busily taking photographs of her. In no mood to play around with the guy, needing someone to take some of her frustrations out on anyway, she stomped out to his van.

The man lowered his camera and tried to look nonchalant, but Sahara wasn't buying his act. "You must be Roam." She reached in through his open window with one hand, opened the van door with the other, and bodily dragged him out into the street. As he protested, she dropped him onto the ground and looked inside the vehicle for the surveillance stuff that he had been using to spy on Bobby.

What she found surprised her. The binoculars he had been using were sitting on the passenger seat, along with a small notebook and a couple of pens. The camera was there as well, perched next to his video recorder. On the floorboard of the passenger side, a cooler sat partly open. Sahara could see that it was loaded with snacks and drinks. "Planning a long stakeout?" She glanced angrily back at the spy.

"You can't go in there!" Roam protested as he scrambled to his feet. "There's sensitive equipment in there; you can't just climb in and start messing with stuff."

Sahara ignored his protests and climbed further into the van. Behind the driving area, every window had at least one video camera pointing out of it and many of them had two. The windows at the very rear of the van had three in each and a complex computer setup was attached to a table bolted to the side of the van that didn't have windows. She looked back out at the man. "What the hell are you doing?"

He grabbed her by a shoe and tried to forcibly pull her from the van. Although Sahara was fairly small, Roam was just plain scrawny and couldn't break her hold on the van's seat. Finally, she hopped out onto the ground.

As he tried to weave past her to get back

in his van, Sahara grabbed him by his shirt. "I think we need to have a talk."

He squeaked and tried to pull out of her grasp but raising a hybrid child had given her the grip strength of a titan. She pulled him across the street and into her shop.

"What are you doing?" he called out to her as the store's door shut behind them. "Are you crazy? This is kidnapping!"

"For starters, you're going to apologize." She dumped him at Bobby's feet. "You've been harassing him and everyone around him and this needs to stop. You owe him an apology."

Roam looked up at her as though he was trying to decide if she was joking. "You can't be serious," he said at last.

"Oh, I'm serious." She folded her arms and waited.

"You know, it's okay," Bobby interjected. "I really should get going, though." He held up the bottle that he had come in for. "How much do I owe you?"

Sahara waved him off. "Don't worry about it. You go ahead and I'll see you next week."

As Bobby moved for the door, the spy tried

to follow him, but Sahara stopped him. "Nope, you're waiting here for a bit. If the closest thing we can get to an apology is a few minutes without you all over him, you're going to be here for a while." She watched out the door as Bobby drove off. "So you might as well relax. Want some tea?"

He blinked up at her in confusion. "Tea?"

"That's what I do here, herbal stuff. So do you want some?"

He watched her, suspicious, as she poured two cups of the complimentary tea she kept on hand for customers. "Is it poisoned?" he asked as she handed him a cup. "Did he come in here to get you to poison me?" He accepted the cup, despite his questions and sniffed at it.

"Nope," she answered as she sat with her own cup and took a sip. "It's just vanilla caramel tea and there's honey of you want it sweetened."

Roam shook his head and tried a sip as well. "If he didn't ask you to poison me then what was he in here for?"

Sahara shook her head. "We aren't here to discuss Bobby; we're here to discuss you."

"Me?" He looked up at her in surprise. "What about me?"

"Well, for starters, why are you stalking people?"

"Stalking? I'm not stalking anyone," he protested. "I'm just after the truth."

"What truth? Bobby said that you had been talking to everyone and I'm sure there were people he hadn't mentioned that you've been bothering also. So why are you so determined to follow him around if you already know what happened?"

He shook his head. "I know what they want people to believe happened." He took another sip of his tea. "Like I said, I'm after the truth, not just the lies that everyone says are the truth."

"So do you do this with every story you come across? At least, all the paranormal ones?"

"There's a lot more going on out there than people know about. Sure, everyone knows about the vampires and werewolves that live everywhere, those are really old news. What I'm interested in is the stuff that people *aren't* talking about." When she raised an eyebrow in question, he explained further. "There are things out there that are so dangerous that people can't know about them, they really couldn't handle it."

"Like what?" she asked as she took another drink of her tea.

"Well, you work with a lot of werewolves, so I'm guessing that you know about the danger classifications system, where all of them are ranked according to how dangerous they are."

"A class one is virtually no threat but it goes up to a class five, which is actively and intentionally killing people."

"That's right. And most of the Weres out in society are classes one and two, right?" When Sahara nodded, he shook his head. "What most people don't realize is that the balance is shifting. Most of the Weres out there right now are actually class two and three and it's creeping over even further. In another couple of months, maybe even as soon as a year, it'll be classes three and four that are the most common."

Sahara wasn't sure she believed that. "Like you said, I deal with a lot of Weres. Most of them that I come across are class one or two."

"Of course they are. You deal with the ones that are actively trying to be good. But even your friend there has jumped up a level." He smiled knowingly at her as he took another sip of his tea.

Sahara thought about that. At least some of what Roam was saying was true; after being caught outside during a lunar event would be enough to shift Bobby from a class one to a class two, at least temporarily. "Just because it happened to one, that doesn't mean it's a widespread thing, though."

"Not by looking at that single case, no. But if you actually look at the registry that the NPIB puts out and you do a comparison, year by year, you can see that the trend is there. I plotted all of the data for the last twenty-three years and ran a linear trend analysis. For the last five years, there has been a slight but steady incline in activity and threat across the board and it's increasing exponentially every year."

He thought for a moment as he took another sip of his tea. "Not that you can believe everything they say, of course, they're trying to hide all of this more than anyone but the information is out there if you know where to look for it."

Strangely, Roam's explanation made an amount of sense to Sahara. "What about beside just the Weres? Is this a trend with all of them?"

"Of course it is." He looked over the rim of his cup at her, one eyebrow raised as though the answer should have been obvious. "I don't know what's causing it but just about every type of paranormal creature out there is be-coming more dangerous. Weres, Vamps, even poltergeists have been acting up more and more lately. Haven't you noticed the number of new response teams that are activated every year? Do you really think that there would be so many new hunters if there wasn't something out there to hunt?

"That's why we need people like me, people who let them know that they're being watched and they aren't going to get away with whatever they're up to." He took a breath, gathering his thoughts. "There have been ten new response teams on the west coast alone this year. Most of them are only certified for one or two types of response: Vamps and Weres, Weres and spirits, you get the idea. But there has been a pretty big push from the government end to increase the response level of each of these teams so that they become global competitors. I even found out that there are a handful of global competitors in place already that are being sent all over the world to respond to class five Vamps and Weres.

"There is even a rumor of some debate about adding a sixth danger level to the classification system as well because of how quickly all of this is escalating but that hasn't been made public yet either."

"What about things that aren't already legal? Have you been hearing anything about that type of thing?" Crazy as Roam seemed, Sahara wouldn't be surprised if he had found something that would turn out to be useful after all. Of course, she wasn't just going to believe what he was saying, the man was a lunatic after all but she could certainly do her own research to confirm if anything he was telling her had any truth to it.

"There are actually a lot of creatures out there that haven't won legalization yet." He took another drink of his tea and frowned at the empty cup. "Course with a lot of those, I really hope they never become legal."

"Like what?" She stood up and poured him some more of the tea. After topping off her own drink she sat back down again. "You've got me curious now." And she was, too. It was no longer just about giving Bobby some time free from Roam's presence. Now she honestly wanted to know if the conspiracy theorist might have something that could help her find Jen.

He shrugged. "There are creatures out there that I don't even know what to call them. Some are worse than others, but some are downright terrifying." He took a drink of his tea and sat back. "I think that the worst of the worst have to be the demons, though."

Sahara blinked at him. "Demons?"

"There were some out here, not too long ago. They killed off a lot of people during the Festival of Souls." After another drink of his tea, he explained. "They looked like giant knights; pictures of them were all over the news. I don't know what they were after but for some reason, the response team kept letting them go. I was going to go check them out, too, and see why they didn't stop the knight things but I couldn't get in to see any of them."

He looked genuinely sad at that but Sahara knew that it was probably a good thing that he hadn't been able to. The team that had been having so much trouble with the knights had been New World Response and Jen had been furious at their inability to stop the murderous creatures. She had taken their threat very personally and more than once had lashed out because of it. Had Roam gone to her and accused her of working with the knights, as it sounded like he believed, Jen probably would have hurt him. Badly.

"But those things, those demons, were stopped. I remember hearing about it on the news."

"I don't know who managed to take them out but it took a while. And the worst part? They weren't even the most dangerous ones in this area."

"They weren't?" she asked. "They seemed pretty dangerous to me."

"Oh, they were pretty dangerous but there

was another demon controlling them. That one, she was pretty bad-ass."

Sahara was stunned. Was he talking about the demoness that had captured Jen? "She?" Ice, an entire river of glacial frost, ran down her spine at the possibility.

Roam nodded. "Seriously hot looking woman, that one. But I doubt she's the only one out there." He looked over at her. "I'm not the only one that knows about them; there've been lots of reports of demonic activity over the last few years and I've just been trying to figure out what they're up to. You know, find out what they want. So when I heard about that she-demon, I had to go check it out."

"And what did you find?" she leaned forward in her seat, eager to find out what Roam knew.

"She lives in this huge house, a pretty decent distance from here. Took me a while to find it, even with all of my research. There's this huge property and you can't even see the house from the road. The place is blocked off by a gate but that was easy enough to climb and I went up there.

"The house is pretty huge, too, and it wasn't

even locked. I went inside to have a look around, and there was this gorgeous woman in there, dressed in these fancy clothes and smiling at me. Scared the hell out of me, it did."

"What happened when she saw you?"

"She started to come towards me, and she was all smiles and stuff, and she tried to tell me what to do, like she was expecting me to just do what she said. I think she was using one of those psychic-type of mind magics on me but I didn't fall for it."

He grinned over at her. "On the one hand, I was curious about what would happen if I just went with her like she was saying she wanted me to. On the other hand, I didn't think I would be able to get away if I went."

"If she's that dangerous, how did you get away?" Sahara was curious. She knew about the mind-control magic the demoness had used and, if Roam was telling the truth, she wanted to know how he wasn't affected by it. Maybe, just maybe, it would help when it was time to get Jen back.

"I have this." He pulled a locket out from under his shirt and held it up for her to see.

Sahara leaned forward to have a better look but it didn't look like anything special. It was a plain, gold-plated locket, with the plating already starting to chip and peel away. There was some engraving in it too, a floral design that looked like daisies. "What's so special about that?" she asked.

"Nothing." He tucked it back under his shirt. "But it has demon's blood inside it and that lets me have protection against demon tricks."

"Where did you get demon's blood?" Sahara had dealt with some questionable suppliers, but she had never heard of anyone peddling in something like that.

He shook his head. "I can't tell you, that's my secret. But it works."

"How?" Sahara wasn't sure she believed him about the blood having some sort of repellant properties against the demonic magic.

"Well, the strength is in the blood and it depends on what type of blood you're using. The more powerful the demon is that you got the blood from, the more resistant you'll be to their magic.

"You see, demons have power classes, just

like everything else. The higher the class ranking the demon is, the more powerful its magic resistance is. In a nutshell, if you get the blood of a powerful demon and keep it with you, then you have some resistance to the lower-classed demons."

He took another sip of his tea and sat back, smirking proudly. "That's something that most people don't ever think of so just about everyone out there is going to fall under their spells."

"So how do you determine how powerful the demon is that you get the blood from, or how powerful other demons are that you encounter?"

He shrugged. "That's not as precise. I've been working on a way to organize them by power levels but there are a lot of them. So far, I only have a very basic structure built."

"You already have a list of demons?" Sahara was amazed. She still thought that Roam's conspiracy theories were a little out of the ordinary but he had a lot more knowledge than she would have expected beneath it all. With a little luck, and possibly a little more tea, she might be able to get some more valuable information out of him.

He nodded. "Like I said, it's a work in progress but it's getting there."

"I don't suppose there's any way I could see it, is there?"

He looked over at her, suspicion evident in his eyes. "What do you want it for?"

She shrugged, trying to look nonchalant. "If they're becoming a bigger problem like you were saying, then it's better to be prepared, isn't it?"

The suspicion faded as he listened. "Finally," he breathed. "Someone who gets it." He downed the last of his tea and stood up. As he headed for the door, he called back over his shoulder, "I'll call you in a day or so when I dig out my records."

Sahara checked her watch. Bobby had been gone long enough that she felt okay about letting Roam go. Plus, now that she had given him something else to focus on, perhaps he would leave the werewolf alone for a little while. "Okay. Do you want a card so you can call me when you're ready?"

Roam stopped, half out the door. "I guess

that would be a good idea, wouldn't it?" He walked over to her counter and pulled one of her business cards out of the display holder. "Just be careful until then. Some of those demons are sneaky and they can pass for human better than some of the humans I've met." He headed back out the door and across the street to his van.

Sahara walked over to the big display window at the front of her shop and watched him leave. As soon as he was out of eyesight, she pulled out her phone and started dialing.

Chapter 5

Todd sat on the floor of Jen's room in the small area that he had cleared out to do his work. Her bed was covered with notes and components along with his spell book and a handful of supplemental scrolls that he hoped would help.

A small, low wooden table sat in the center of the clearing. It held a few partially-burned candles, a small pot that was filled with a bubbling, foul-smelling mixture, a square of ceramic that held some smoldering herbs, and an empty coffee cup that read "*Instant Human, Just Add Coffee.*" He sighed as the ball of clear crystal that he held in the smoke refused to reveal anything.

It was a specially-ordered ball that he had

custom-tuned to his sister's resonance. Every other time he had used it to check in on her, it had required almost no effort on his part. Now, however, it refused to tell him anything.

Resisting the urge to smash the four-thousand-dollar crystal against the far wall, he set the ball back into its protective case and set it aside. He took a deep calming breath as he tried to rearrange his thoughts and settle his nerves. Contrary to what most people believed, his sister didn't have a worse temper than he did. If anything, she was calmer. He exhaled slowly and looked at his gathered implements. Apparently, he was going to need something stronger. He reached behind him and pulled his book from the clutter on the bed and began to flip pages.

He had been working on tracking where she had been taken for almost two weeks, since the night she had been kidnapped. The strain of that much magical effort was starting to get to him and the lack of sleep wasn't helping either. There was no doubt that what he really needed was a good night's sleep but every time he tried to rest, his mind was filled with images of his twin sister, screaming for help.

He flipped past a teleportation spell and briefly wondered if he would be able to step to where she was, grab her and bring her back but then he remembered that he had to have a lock on where she was before that particular spell would work. Since he still wasn't even able to verify that she was alive, despite his refusal to consider otherwise, the teleportation wouldn't take.

As the smoke from the herbs cleared, he sat back against the side of the bed and pulled out his phone. He had already been gone from work longer than he had intended but he wasn't going anywhere until his sister came home. He dialed a familiar number and after only a couple of transfers his supervisor answered the phone.

"Hey, Matt, this is Todd Rice."

"Hey, Todd, how's the vacation going?"

"Not so well," Todd explained. "We're having a bit of a family crisis out here so I'm not going to be back to the office when I had planned."

"Family crisis, huh? Okay, you go ahead and

take however long you need. Just keep me informed, okay?"

"Can do. Could you transfer me over to Chris's office? I was supposed to start giving him a lift in when I got back, so I need to let him know what's going on."

"No problem," Matt answered. "Just hang on a second."

As he was waiting to be transferred, Todd flipped another page in his spell book. He had looked over his planar travel spell at least a dozen times before but always with the same sense of apprehension. He hadn't ever tried that spell before and wasn't entirely convinced that he was powerful enough to control it if he did.

"Hey, buddy, where are you?" Chris Knox, one of Todd's closest friends at Viceroy, picked up the phone. "Boss said you hadn't gotten back to town yet."

"Nope, I'm still out on the west coast. Are you on a secure line?"

"Of course," Chris answered, confusion apparent in his voice. "What's going on?"

"It's Jen." Chris Knox was more than just a

coworker to Todd. When he had first started at the Academy, Chris had been the first friend Todd made and the pair had been the best of friends ever since. They had been through plenty of hairy situations and Todd knew that his friend could be trusted with the truth. "She was kidnapped and I'm trying to find her. But you've got to keep this under your hat, okay?"

"Yeah, no problem. What happened?" Chris's voice turned serious, recognizing the gravity of Todd's situation.

Todd explained about how Jen and her team had gone after a demon and that another demon had taken his sister. "We don't know where she was taken to and none of my spells are working to find her."

"Damn, dude, I'm sorry. What can I do to help?"

"First of all, you can keep this quiet. There's already NPIB sniffing around out here and I want to keep them as far away from her as I can, at least until we have her back and I know she's okay."

"That makes sense, especially after the Ravenwood fiasco." Just over ten years ago,

Harold Ravenwood had accidentally been transported to Derathim while casting a planar travel spell, similar to the one in Todd's spell book. When Ravenwood managed to find his way back after almost a week trapped on the dark plane, the NPIB had whisked him away. By the time they were finished running all of their tests, trying to see how badly that much immersion in dark energy had affected him in an attempt to assess the long-term damage people would expect to receive after Derathic energy exposure, Ravenwood hadn't known who he was anymore.

Harold Ravenwood had lived the last ten years in a mental institution, heavily medicated because of the hallucinations and other lasting effects that he suffered from as a result of the tests that had been performed on him. A far cry from the Academy President and respected mage he had once been, Ravenwood now depended on a team of caretakers for his very survival.

"Yeah, that's what we're trying to avoid here. But like I said, none of my location spells will show her, not even her scrying ball. So I'm trying to think of something, anything that will have a better chance of finding her."

Chris thought for a moment, and Todd could hear him flipping pages, presumably in his own spell book. "What types of things are you using to locate her? Clothes, stuff like that?"

"Yeah, pretty much. I have her clothes, her favorite coffee cup, and her pillow, all of that stuff."

"And none of that's working? Let me see." He flipped some more pages. "What about stuff that's even more personal?"

"Like what?"

"Like toothbrush, hairs out of her hairbrush. Things that would only have her on them. They hold more of a person's essence than just a pillow or a shirt. Do you have any of that type of thing?"

"I'm sure I do somewhere." Todd got up and walked across the room to the dresser. He opened the top drawer and discovered that Jen still kept her hair stuff in the same place she had since they were kids. "I have her hairbrush. I'll go ahead and try that, thank you."

"No problem. I'll keep digging out here, see if there's anything else I can come up with."

After getting off the phone, Todd stood up and stretched. He had been sitting on the ground a little too long and his legs and lower back were stiff but he didn't have time to go for a good long run and work everything loose again. He dug through his knapsack, looking for some new components to try the spells again. As he dug through the hairbrush, he noticed that there were a lot of loose hairs in it and he was glad that Jen didn't regularly clean out her toiletries.

While he was thinking about it, he left the bedroom and went to check for a toothbrush in the bathroom. In one of the drawers, he found her dental care supplies and carried all of them back to the bedroom with him. Before getting started in his spellcasting, however, he needed to go find something to eat. With the way his stomach was complaining, there was no way he would be able to focus enough to cast anything successfully.

He headed out to the kitchen, certain that there would be food of some variety in the fridge. Mary had always cooked when she was stressed, so the fridge had been bursting at the seams for a while now. He popped containers open and loaded a plate with pasta, carrots, and ravioli that was stuffed with something, he just wasn't sure what. Not that it really mattered, in the end food was food.

After heating it all in the microwave, he sat at the kitchen table to eat and think. Jaime was out in the living room, tapping at the keyboard of her laptop. Her job in the advertising department of a clothing retailer let her work from pretty much anywhere, so she wasn't losing out on her work while she was away from home. He wasn't sure where Mary was but he suspected that she was out at the grocery store again, probably looking for ingredients for yet another recipe she wanted to try. Troy and Patrick had left earlier that morning to help the New World Response team with some sort of vampire problem they were having and hadn't returned yet. Todd hoped that they weren't in any sort of trouble; he wasn't sure how much more trouble he could handle right then.

Todd knew that he wasn't doing well. He had

known about the hairs in the hairbrush, it was one of the basic tricks they had learned in their first year of the Academy but he had forgotten. He hadn't quite been thinking right the whole time Jen had been gone and he didn't like the feeling. The gnawing ache that had appeared in the center of his stomach the first time he had been told of his sister's kidnapping had refused to lessen with time. If anything, it had only gotten worse.

He also suspected that his faltering concentration was a big part of why he hadn't been able to find her yet, which he liked even less.

As he ate, Jaime finished what she was working on and came in to check on him. "No progress yet?" she asked as she sat across the table from him.

Todd shook his head. "Still nothing but I talked to a friend and he reminded me of another trick I can try."

Jaime sighed and lowered her eyes. "I know none of us wants to talk about this but what if we aren't able to find her?"

"We will," Todd insisted.

"I know we're doing everything we can but

it's been two weeks now and we aren't any closer than we were when we started. What happens when we run completely out of bright ideas?" She reached out to take his hand. "Look, this isn't easy for me, either. But wouldn't it be better to call in the big guns?"

He knew what she was asking. Todd was a researcher at Viceroy, the largest magical research facility on the planet. His company employed thousands of mages who had worked with the company for decades, some even longer. The oldest and most powerful of the mages, the Venerali Magii, tended to live for hundreds of years, a conservative estimate in Todd's opinion. His own magical skill, impressive as it was, didn't hold a candle to even the lowest of the Venerali Magii.

Todd shook his head. "Not unless we have to. If I call the Venerali, they'll come out and take the whole thing over and we'll never know what they find, if anything."

"Why wouldn't they?"

Todd shrugged. "That's just the way they work. If the Venerali Magii get involved and if they find Jen on the dark plane, they'll keep her. She's been to another plane and they'll want to keep her for a while." He took another bite of his food. "Probably for studies on how non-magical people react to planar travel, or something stupid like that." His brows furled in frustration. "Research is what we do, after all."

"But wouldn't that be better than not getting her back at all? Her being stuck wherever she is?"

"Not necessarily," Todd pointed out. "Either way, she'll be assumed to be tainted by dark energy and they'll want to cleanse her." He shuddered at the thought. "Trust me; it's not a nice process."

"How do you know they'll keep her?" Jaime asked. "They might give her back to us."

"Because it's happened before," Todd explained. Ravenwood was hardly the first person to be to Derathim and back. He was simply the most publicized; a cautionary tale for Academy students.

That piece of news sat Jaime back. "It has?" Her surprise was not unexpected. Not many people who hadn't been through some sort of magical training knew the story of Ravenwood.

For obvious reasons, it wasn't something that the magic-using population frequently discussed.

Todd nodded solemnly. "And I don't want to see that happen to Jen." He stood up and put his dishes into the sink. "I should get back to it."

He locked himself back in Jen's bedroom and sat in front of his worktable. He pulled out the hairs he had found in Jen's hairbrush and hoped that they would be enough to find her.

Twenty grueling minutes later, he blinked in surprise as his scrying ball lit from within. The glow was dim and he could barely make out any shapes but he knew that it meant that Jen was alive, somewhere and that he could get to her. The knot in his stomach contracted sharply as he recognized what he was looking at.

She was alive.

His sister was still alive.

He jumped to his feet and ran out to the living room, almost breaking the lock on the bedroom door in his haste to get out and report the exciting news to the rest of the gathered friends and family. He carried the still-flickering ball with him, stepping carefully and whispering words of encouragement to the hazy light.

When he got to the living room, he discovered that Mary had returned, as had Troy and Patrick. A whoop of joy tore from his throat as he skidded into the room and held the ball above his head in triumph. "I found her!" he shouted.

Everyone sprang to their feet and clambered around him, eager to see what the crystal ball would reveal. It hadn't cleared up much since it started to flicker but Todd's hopes were high. "She's alive, we know that for sure," he explained to the group. "I'm not sure where she's at yet but she's alive!"

"But can you find her?" Patrick asked as he peered into the ball's depths. "Will this thing show us how to get to her?"

"Right now, no. But I found something that'll work, so I should be able to get a better set up and running soon." He looked around the group, his face glowing with excitement. "But most of my spells require that I can find her, so I've got that now."

"So where is she?" Troy asked. "I mean, do you have at least a general idea?"

Todd's grin faded just a bit. "Sort of. It looks like she's not on the same plane as we are but that was what we were assuming already. Now I just need to build a way to get us there, wherever she is, or to get her back here."

As the light in the ball slowly faded, Jaime looked at her brother. "So what are you waiting for, then?"

Todd blinked at her. "I don't know; what am I waiting for?" He turned back towards the bedroom. "Hey Patrick," he called over his shoulder as he half-jogged down the hallway. "Do you think you can get me a really big mirror?"

"Like how big?" Patrick called back.

"I don't know, big enough to walk through."

Patrick only thought for a brief second before responding. "I will. Not sure where but I will." He turned to Troy. "Come on, let's go." Dragging the hybrid by an arm, he headed for the door.

Back in the bedroom, Todd started to scoop up his supplies and cart them out to the living room. If he was going to have to use the planar travel spell after all, he would need a lot more space to work in.

As he carried his supplies, he realized that there was a huge risk in him using that spell. Planar travel was one of the most difficult spells he had come across and if he messed it up there was a good chance that things could go very, very wrong. He should have had at least another two years' worth of training before using it, before even considering it really, but Jen was worth whatever might happen.

He had to try.

Once he had all of his equipment out in the living room, he started organizing it so that he could discover which components he already had and what he would still have to go find. He had known about the mirror, so he had at least been able to send Troy and Patrick out after that and get them doing something instead of hanging over him and trying to be helpful. Besides, given what Patrick did for work, he was the most likely person that Todd could think of who would know where to find a mirror big enough to suit their magical needs.

He still had concerns about the spell. Not

only did he not have enough components and equipment with him to cast it, he knew that if he cast it wrong, there was a possibility that he wouldn't survive the backlash from it. The spell to open a portal like that really should require two people to cast it, at a minimum. Doing it himself with no other assistance was almost unheard-of at his current power level. It would use a tremendous amount of energy to build and hold a portal of that magnitude and if that energy escaped, the blast could kill him before he would be able to regain control of it.

And that was being optimistic.

If things went really wrong, there was more than simply his own life and the possible rescue of his sister at stake. Not only could the backlash kill or seriously injure anyone who happened to be near him while he was casting, the energy could conceivably go through the portal to injure whoever – or whatever – was on the other side. If it was the demon who would get hurt as a result, he could live with that but if Jen's life was on the line, there was nothing he wanted less than to bring her even more harm than what had already befallen her.

While he set out all of his gear, he tried to keep his expression neutral. He knew that if his family knew how dangerous this magic was, they would probably try to talk him out of it. Years of playing poker with Chris after classes had served him well for keeping anyone from being able to read his thoughts across his face. Granted, there were a number of other people who he knew could cast a planar travel spell and had done so in the past successfully but he didn't trust any of them. Not completely.

Definitely not where his sister was involved.

He was almost finished setting out all of his implements when Patrick and Troy returned. They were lugging the largest mirror that Todd had ever seen into the house, which surprised him. "That's even bigger than the one at the Academy," he said when they uncovered it.

"You said you wanted a big one," Troy explained. "This was the biggest one we could find."

The pair leaned the mirror, which was easily twelve feet across and over seven feet tall, against a wall. It was almost too tall to stand up straight but it cleared the ceiling by less than an inch once they had it placed.

It wasn't all mirror, Todd quickly discovered when he came over to have a closer look. There was a thick frame around it, adding to its already massive size. The glass was clear, however, and there were no warps or dings in it, which were the most important characteristics that Todd was looking for. Most people believed that any sort of mirror could be used for magical working, but Todd knew better. Even the slightest imperfection in the reflective surface could cause the spell to fail. That was one of the reasons that magical shops charged so much for their mirrors. They were guaranteed to be blemish-free.

"Will that work?" Patrick asked as Todd inspected the mirror.

"Looks like it. Where did you find this thing?"

He shrugged. "One of the guys we're dealing with at work was talking about it the other day. He had wanted a mirrored wall about this size but he decided that he would rather have it in smaller panels so he turned down the delivery. Since it's so huge, I figured the chances were good that it hadn't sold already, and I was right."

Todd nodded. "I can imagine."

"So how long before we go get her?" Troy asked, his eyes bright with eagerness.

"Not for a little while yet," Todd answered. "I don't have all the components here that I need, so I have to go get them still. Plus," he added, "I still need to read through the spell a bunch of times and get the mirror ready to be used as an implement."

"So how long?" From his posture, Troy looked as though he was ready to leap through the mirror that moment. Not that Todd could blame the hybrid; he wished everything was ready to go too.

He sighed. "Probably a few days."

Everyone's faces fell at his announcement. "I thought it'd be sooner than that," Jaime pointed out.

"Sorry," Todd said, "but these things take time and the bigger the spell, the more prep time it takes."

"Components," Mary piped in. "Are those like

ingredients?" When Todd nodded, she asked, "Can we help you get them?"

Todd thought for a moment. "I suppose so," he agreed. "At least, some of them you can get. There are still a few that I'll have to get by myself."

He wrote out a list of the components that they would be able to find and handed it over to her. "Just get whatever you can," he explained. "If you can't find something, or if you aren't sure about something, I can take care of it."

She and Jaime divided up the list and headed for the door.

Once they were gone, Troy looked over at Todd. "What can we do to help?"

"Well," Todd thought for a moment. "If you can find some window cleaner, the mirror has to be as clean as possible before I start working on it."

Troy headed for the kitchen to look for glass cleaner. While he was digging, Patrick looked over at Todd. "Peppermints?"

"That would be wonderful." While he was still in the Academy, Todd had discovered that he got really tired any time he was using a challenging spell. Not that there was any surprise there; any challenging spell was taxing on the caster. After almost a year of trial-and-error, he discovered that sucking on peppermint candy helped to keep him focused and made his spell work a lot easier. It was a technique that he still used occasionally and he was surprised that Patrick had remembered.

As Patrick gave him a knowing look while walking towards the door, Todd realized what he had just admitted. He just hoped that his brother would keep it quiet.

The last thing they needed was to have everyone being concerned about whether the spell would work.

Chapter 6

The room was spinning but it had been doing that the whole time she had been there. As Jen opened her eyes, she tried to think back on how long she had been in these awful rooms but she couldn't quite wrap her brain into coherent thought. The rough stone floor was cool against her skin, even though the air in the room was fairly warm. Her cheek stuck to something sticky as she tried to lift her head and she wondered how much of the gluey substance was residue of her own blood.

Even though the room was too dark to actually see much, she knew that she wasn't alone. She could see dim shapes, darker shadows in the already black room. Others were being held there as well, all of them as battered as she was. At least she wasn't in a cage anymore, she thought to herself as she tried unsuccessfully to get her eyes to focus. As she lifted a hand to her face, she remembered why she was so groggy.

Everywhere was inflamed; both of her eyes were swollen almost shut and blood had dried beneath her nose and on her lips. She could still feel the blow that had knocked her out, it was the last thing she could remember before waking up. As she rolled to her side, she reflexively winced in pain and remembered that her arms had both taken a beating as well. There was only so long she could hang suspended by her wrists before the shoulders popped out of their sockets. At least neither of them was broken and she took some solace in that thought. There had been a few times when she had thought her tormentors had pushed her far enough to snap bones but so far they hadn't. The beatings were getting worse every day she was stuck in that hellhole and she knew that it was only a matter of time before she started taking damage that would be irreversible.

Nearby, she could hear the others breathing.

Some were asleep but she doubted that all of them were. As the pain seared through her veins, the fog in her head started to clear and she wondered how long she had been unconscious that time. Hours, she thought, at the very least. Possibly even days.

When she sat up, the chain that attached the collar around her neck to the stone wall behind her rattled slightly and she could feel its weight drag her down. Knowing it had to be done but dreading it all the same, she heaved herself to a crouched position, as close to standing as the leash allowed, and took a deep breath. As she threw herself onto the ground, she angled her body to land on one shoulder, the only way she had discovered to put the joint back into place.

She rolled to her back, whimpering in agony as even more pain coursed through her. Even as she gasped for air and bit back howls of misery, she took pride in the fact that she had grown stronger, even in these dire circumstances. The first time she had put her shoulder back into place, she had passed out from the pain. Now, she was fairly certain that she could survive both of them and stay conscious.

Once the pain subsided enough to let her move again, she rolled to her knees and pushed herself onto her feet once more, this time aiming for the other shoulder.

"You know they're just going to pull them back out again," a voice whispered to her from the darkness. She recognized it as belonging to Jon, one of the other slaves trapped in the small room with her.

"I know, but I can't just let it be," she answered as she pulled herself up to a sitting position again. "How long was I out this time?"

She could see the dim outline of him as he moved to sit up while they spoke. Jon was a large man, probably taller than six feet, and broad in the shoulders. It was hard to tell much more than that in their cramped, dimly-lit surroundings and when they were brought in and out of the room there were more important things to focus on than the physical characteristics of the people around her. "Only about an hour," he answered. "They took Christy out when they brought you in."

Jen swore under her breath. This room, with everyone living in darkness and chained to either the walls or the floor, was a four-star resort compared to the living nightmare in the next room over. "I'd hoped they wouldn't have wanted to play any more after they were done with me."

Jon chuckled, but it was without mirth. "Do you really believe that anything you could do would get them to stop?"

"One can always try," Jen grunted as she pulled her legs under her. Everything was sore and it felt like she was covered with abrasions on every inch of her skin. "How are you guys holding up?"

Most of the people in the holding cell, as Jen had come to think of it, had been there longer than Jen had. Some of them were willing to talk and had no problem explaining the daily routine to her but there were others who were already so broken that they wouldn't even acknowledge that there were other people in the room. Jen suspected that these people were evidence of the demons' ultimate goals; as soon as someone became that damaged, the demons decided that they weren't fun anymore.

Demons had a much different idea of fun

than Jen had but she had started to get the gist of their amusement.

"We're okay," Jon answered. "Bailey's still recovering from his turn the other day but it looks like he's going to be okay."

Jen swore under her breath. Everyone agreed that Bailey had been a captive of the demons longer than any of the others, and to Jen it looked like he was getting closer and closer to the breaking point every day. She wasn't sure how much longer he would be able to keep it together. Jen had never been a fan of abuse and her inability to stop what the demons were doing to everyone only stoked the fires of rage that burned inside her.

One of the things that had surprised her was that she had only seen male demons. She remembered the demoness who had engineered her capture but hadn't seen her since arriving. Every now and again she entertained the idea that her team had somehow managed to take her out and escape the mental grasp she had over them but she doubted it. The demoness's hold over them had been strong enough to force Joel, a man who had been one of her closest friends for almost ten years, to attempt to cut out her heart. If she could make them do that, there wasn't much of a limit to what else she could make them do.

She felt along the floor as far as the chains would let her, as she had done every day that she had been imprisoned. She didn't know what she was looking for, perhaps a loose chunk of rock that would work as a weapon or maybe even a key to the locks that had been dropped, unnoticed, by one of her demon captors.

When her search of the floor turned up nothing, as usual, she turned to the wall. She tested the ring where the chain was attached to the stone, tugging on it in the vain hope that she had somehow managed to work it loose and it would tug free this time. As always, it held firm.

She explored the lock that kept the chain in place and wished again that she had one of Troy's lock picking tools. Her fingers traveled up the chain, exploring every link between the wall and her collar, looking for any sign of weakness where she might be able to tug free. Finally, she examined the collar itself, feeling around the thick, rough leather. The collar was held in place by a smaller lock but as many times as she tugged, yanked, and wrenched on it, the most she managed to do was further abrade her own neck.

"You need to stop doing that," another voice chimed in. "They're going to kill you if you don't start to behave."

"No, if they were going to kill me, they would have already done it," Jen grunted as she continued to yank on her restraints. "They want something else; I just don't know what." She thought for a moment. "Zack?" She thought she recognized the second voice but she didn't have everyone's names quite down yet.

"Yeah."

Unlike Jon, Zack hadn't sat up to talk with her. He remained prone on the ground and Jen had recognized a few days ago that most of the group refused to get up unless they were selected as entertainment. She knew that it was driven by self-preservation because if you were lying down like everyone else when the demons came in, you were less likely to be singled out. Considering how small Zack was, she couldn't blame him for not wanting to draw attention to himself.

The demons weren't very selective about who they played with.

Jen, on the other hand, would rather be selected herself than have to sit and do nothing while one of the other captives was tortured. Not that she enjoyed being the plaything of a demon but she would rather take the brunt of their wrath onto herself than have to listen to one of the others beg for mercy that wouldn't be given.

The demons seemed more than willing to go along with her on that because every time they noticed she was awake she was selected to be taken out of the room. As much as she hated the beatings, she was glad every time she was selected. The more times she was taken out of the room, the fewer times everyone else would be. It wasn't much but for now it was the best that she could do.

A couple of times, the demons had appeared to be impressed with how quickly she was recovering from her injuries. Even though they spoke among themselves in their own language, she had started to pick up bits and pieces, words and phrases that were used more frequently. She hadn't let on that she was starting to understand what they were saying to each other because she knew that, at some point, she might be able to use that knowledge to escape. If they knew that she understood them, they would probably just stop talking in front of her and she wouldn't be able to follow what was going on.

She still wasn't sure how she would be able to use this stolen knowledge but she would find a way. As Todd always said, knowledge is power. She just needed to figure out a way to use that power to escape.

As far as the increased healing rate, Jen wasn't sure how she was healing as fast as she was but she had to admit that it was real. After a few of the beatings she had received, she had been certain that she was about to die, only to wake a number of hours later, more or less whole. Today was just another case of that. She knew that the demons had damaged her fairly severely but for some reason she was able to move everything and was actually not in very much pain, at least not as much as she figured she should have been.

"Besides, if they take me out there, that means that they don't take any of you out there."

"But that's crazy," Zack argued quietly. "Sooner or later, they're going to mess you up even worse than they already have."

Jen shook her head, but then realized that they couldn't see her any better than she could see them. "They haven't done anything that I haven't been able to recover from."

"You're doing what?" Jon asked, his voice incredulous. "Why would you take the hit for us?"

"I don't know why but I seem to be healing faster than I should." She licked the last of the blood from her lips. When she checked, she discovered that the cuts were already healed. The swelling over her eyes had gone down too, as she discovered when she lifted a hand to feel her face again.

She stopped and looked over towards the men. "Strange question," she said. "Have they asked you for anything?"

There was a moment of silence before Jon

spoke up. "Not that I know of but I don't understand what they are saying when they talk."

"They haven't asked you to accept them, or
something like that?"

"Accept them?" Zack asked. "What's that
supposed to mean?"

"I have no idea. But one of them keeps telling
me that I need to accept him and I wasn't sure
what it meant either." She sighed and leaned
back against the cold wall. "I was hoping one of
you might know."

"Shh," Jon interrupted before anything more
could be said. "I think someone's coming." He
lowered herself to the floor and lay motionless,
the same as everyone else did, except Jen. If
she was to lie down, the demons might think
she was still unconscious and take one of the
others instead of her. She sat, her back against
the wall, and waited.

A light turned on at the far end of the
room and Jen watched as one of her tormentors
brought a woman, crawling on all fours, into the
room. She had blond hair, tangled and dingy
from not being washed, and bruises covering

most of her body. Jen was relieved to see that they hadn't hurt Christy too badly, after all.

Jen recognized the demon leading the woman into the room; he was some sort of apprentice to the demon that had brought Jen to this awful place. Although she only understood a little of what the demons said to each other, she believed that this one was called Cylin.

For the most part, Jen was brought out for the entertainment of Thaxter, the demon that had claimed her, but there had been times that she and some of the others were brought out to entertain Cylin. There had also been mention of another demon, this one called Vanitha, but Jen hadn't seen that one yet. Perhaps it was the demoness who had captured her. If that was the case, the other demons didn't seem to know what had become of her, either.

Cylin was tall, as all of the demons seemed to be. He had long dark hair, not quite black but only a shade or two away from it. His skin was slightly tanned as though he spent a lot of time in the sun. His eyes were bright sea green but completely devoid of any emotion.

The demon led Christy by her collar chain

over to a wall near Jen and attached her to a wall hook. As he turned to head for another victim, he looked down and met Jen's eyes. "Ah, I see you're awake."

Jen watched quietly as the demon changed direction and walked over toward her. He unhooked her chain from the wall and started to drag her towards the door. "The master will be pleased to see that you are ready to play again so soon." His voice was accented slightly, another hint about his natural language.

As always, Jen refused to crawl, so her feet and knees were scraped and bleeding by the time they reached the smooth stone floor beyond the door. The demon dragging her didn't slow at the blood but pulled her over to a pair of chains that were hanging from the ceiling next to a wall. He stepped on her leash to hold her in place as he lowered the chains and attached the cuffs that were suspended at the ends to each of her wrists.

As she was hoisted into the air, she squinted against the blinding light. Her eyes had adjusted for the barely-present light in the holding cell so the light in this room, as low as it was, still stung her eyes. When she was finally vertical and dangling a couple of inches off the ground, Cylin attached more cuffs to her ankles and chained them to hooks in the floor. As her eyes adjusted, Jen looked around the dreaded room.

The floor and walls were made of smooth grey stones that had smears of black through them, as though they had been absorbing all of the blood that had been spilled and were now stained a darker hue. The room was lit by a series of wall sconces, placed a few feet apart on all four of the walls. Every sconce had a light burning in it, and she stifled a whimper as she remembered the last time she had been pressed against one of the hot lamps. Thankfully, this time she had been suspended between sconces so the wall was cool on her back instead of blazing hot.

There was a rolling rack of tools that the demons pulled to where they needed it, which looked like a pair of chalkboards set back-to-back with the bases separated a bit so that they leaned against each other. The boards weren't for chalk, however, as they held rows upon rows of hooks from which they hung their nefarious devices.

A doorway led out of the far end of the torture room and Jen had often wondered where it led to, if it would be a path of escape when she was finally able to break free of her chains and make a run for it. This was the entrance that the demons used when they left or entered the room any of the times that Jen had been brought forth and she was sure that beyond that exit was where they kept the rest of their torturous equipment.

Usually when Jen was brought to the torture room, she was the only person there besides one or both of the demons. This time, however, there was another person already hooked up to a low table that was covered in what appeared to be black leather. He lay flat on his back, arms and legs chained to the floor beyond each of the table's corners. Welts covered him everywhere that Jen could see, and there were angry bruises from his toes to his violet hair. His face was turned away from her so she couldn't see his face, but it didn't matter. No matter who he was, he didn't deserve what they had done to him. She watched him for a moment and discovered that his chest was rising and falling as he breathed, so at least he was still alive. It didn't appear that he was conscious, probably a relief given the amount of damage he had obviously received.

The demon pulled the rack of implements to the center of the room and settled it where he wanted it before coming back over to Jen. He unhooked her feet from the floor, flipped a lever on the wall beneath one of the sconces, and pulled her by her leash toward the center of the room. The chains that held her upright moved along the tracks that crisscrossed the ceiling. They had been used to move her from one place to another many times before, so the motion didn't surprise her.

In the center of the room, Cylin reattached her ankles to the floor and, certain that she was secure, pulled a whip off the rack. It was long and narrow, one that he had used on her plenty of times before but Jen held her face expressionless, not wanting to give him the satisfaction of a response even though she was already cringing inside.

As the stiff leather cracked across her back, she stifled a cry of pain, biting her lower lip to hold it in as long as she could. It was the same thing she always did and even though she knew that she would be beaten until long after her mouth was bleeding, she held out for as long as she could.

The demon continued to strike, lashing her from her feet to her shoulders before working his way around to stand in front of her. He covered her sides and her arms in welts and she could feel the blood begin to trickle down her lips as Cylin continued whipping her until every inch of her skin was on fire. Her feet, her inner thighs, even her neck were soon covered in welts and Jen felt as though she was being painted by a psychotic artist whose preferred medium was lava. Tears streaked her face and she bit her lips again, trying to use one pain to block out the rest, not very successfully.

She had no idea how long the beating continued. All she knew was that the only thing still holding her up was the chains attached to the ceiling; she no longer had enough strength left in her legs to support her own weight by the time the demented demon stopped.

"Are you ready to submit to us?" Cylin leaned forward to whisper into her ear. "Will you accept us and submit to our desires?"

The questions were the same that she was asked every time she had been brought into the torture room. If it wasn't Cylin asking them, it was Thaxter, his master. As she had every other time, Jen shook her head to the demon's questions. She opened an eye as he asked, however, thankful that there was at least a momentary pause in the beating. Cylin had turned back to his rack of devices, so she took the opportunity to look over at the man on the table, who had turned to face her. Apparently he was conscious after all.

His eyes were as violet as his hair and she wondered if he had dyed it to match or if he was under an illusion spell. Her brother had played with illusions while he was in training so she wondered if this newest captive was a mage as well. Tears streaked down his face as he looked at her, and when their eyes met, he silently mouthed the words, "I'm sorry," to her.

For a moment, Jen wondered what he had to be sorry for. She hadn't ever seen him before, as far as she could tell, so he couldn't have done anything to her. Maybe he felt responsible for her being brought in to join the party. If that was the case, she would reassure him about it later.

Cylin turned his attention to her again, yet another implement of pain in his hand, this one consisting of tightly knotted chains. He stepped around her and she closed her eyes. He had used the same device on her enough times to know that it increased the pain from the lashing exponentially. She had to hand it to the demons: when it came to beating people, they knew their stuff.

He circled her with the weapon, covering her already-welted skin with fresh marks. Jen whimpered with every blow and with each strike of the chains she was certain that her arms would rip completely free of their sockets and she would be sent sprawling to the floor. Blood ran freely down over her chin and she couldn't find a good place on her lower lip to bite.

She heard the other prisoner calling out to

the demon, asking Cylin to stop, but the demon ignored his pleas. Jen wanted to reassure him, to let him know that she was all right but she was afraid that if she opened her eyes and tried to speak, her resolve would crack and she would end up begging for mercy as well.

When the demon finally tired of the savage beating, Jen hung limply at the end of her tethers. She gasped for air and spat out the blood that had collected in her mouth. Although she had aimed for Cylin when she spat, the demon wasn't quite close enough to hit. Apparently he had learned from the times he had stood too close, as this wasn't the first time she had tried to spit at him.

As he hung the weapon back no its rack among the whips and other devices, the demon laughed at her antics. "It seems there is still some fire in you yet." He looked over his shoulder at her. "Are you ready to accept us and submit? When you accept us, this will all stop. Are you that determined to keep this punishment going?"

She grinned at him, baring her bloody teeth

and lowering her eyebrows. "If you wanted someone easy, you should have gotten a hooker."

Anger showed on the demon's face for the first time during that session. "You will give in to us and accept us. Make no mistake on that."

Her grin didn't falter as she met his eyes. "You know what I'm looking forward to?" she chuckled. "The day I get to kill you." Her grin faded, but her eyes remained steely. "And I will enjoy it; I want you to know that."

Only moments later, she found herself sliding across the smooth stone floor as the demon dragged her back to the dark room, done with her torture for the time being. Her tears mixed with her blood, leaving a trail from the wall of the torture room to the wall in the holding cell, where the demon reattached her leash to its hook and turned to select another plaything.

She leaned back against the wall, letting the cool stone soothe her inflamed back as the violet-haired man was dragged into the holding cell as well. Thankfully the demon hadn't continued toying with him after finishing with her. She had to stay strong; if she succumbed to the stress, she wouldn't be able to find a way out of this awful place. She still wasn't sure how she was going to do it but as the pain subsided and she felt herself drifting off to sleep, she remembered that she knew of someone who might be able to help.

That night, she called out to the dreamwalker.

Chapter 7

Sahara was just starting to wonder if Roam was ever going to call her back. It had been almost two days since he had left and she hadn't heard a word from him since. She puttered around her shop until closing time when she shut everything down and headed for home. At the very least, she told herself, Roam hadn't been bothering Bobby since she had interfered. She had spoken to the Were earlier that day and he hadn't heard anything from the paranoid conspiracy theorist either. At the very least, he hadn't been as fixated on Bobby as he had previously been, which was a relief.

On the drive home, she stopped at the grocery store to pick up some milk, apples, and something quick to make for dinner. When she spotted the family-sized boxes of corn dogs, she smiled to herself and dropped the box into her cart. The kids were going to be happy tonight.

When she got back to her house, she found Joel and the kids parked in front of the television, watching cartoons. She checked to make sure that it was a regular cartoon that the kids were allowed to watch and not one of Joel's more mature anime movies. Satisfied that the show was family-friendly, she went into the kitchen to start dinner.

Just as they sat down for a delicious meal of corn dogs and frozen potato nuggets, her phone rang. She didn't recognize the number, so she stepped away from the table to answer it. "Hello?"

"Hey, Sahara, this is Roam, remember me?"

"Of course, I remember you. How's it going?"

"Not too bad," he answered. "Were you still interested in looking at the information I have on demons?"

"Yeah, I am. In fact, I was just wondering if you were going to call me back about that." What she had really been expecting was for the man to call her at Sugar and Spice. She had no idea how he had gotten her personal number but decided not to press the point. If he had something useful for her, it was worth it.

"Good, I wasn't sure if you were honestly wanting to know, trying to distract me from your werewolf friend, or just trying to be nice." The relief sounded in his voice and Sahara wondered again what she had gotten into. No matter, she had decided to see what he knew and playing along with his paranoia seemed to be the only way she was going to find out.

"I'm not sure where to meet you," he explained. "I have everything on demons here in my van but I think your shop's closed and I don't know of anywhere else that would work for us to meet."

For a moment, she entertained the idea of inviting him over but quickly dismissed the thought. As nuts as Roam was, she wasn't sure she wanted him to know where she lived. Having her phone number was bad enough. "I can meet you at the shop," she volunteered. "I do have a key, after all." She chuckled as she spoke. Sugar and Spice was one of the most neutral places she could think of and it was only a couple of blocks from the police station, so she would be safe there. Especially since she knew that Joel was listening and would know where she was going. "Say, half an hour?"

"Sounds good," Roam agreed. "I guess I'll see you there."

She got off the phone and walked back over to the table. "It's the guy I told you about," she explained to her husband as she picked up a corn dog from her plate and took a bite. "He says he has all his info in his van, so I'm meeting him at the shop to go through it all."

"Do you really think this'll turn up anything?"

She shrugged and popped a potato nugget into her mouth. "Only one way to find out."

"Just be careful," he warned her. "I'll call you every half hour. If you don't answer, I'm calling the police."

Normally Sahara would be frustrated by his over-protectiveness but with everything that had happened she couldn't fault him this time. She knew that she was putting herself into a dangerous situation; the only question was how dangerous it would turn out to be. "I'll be careful," she promised. "And if anything happens, I'll call." She picked up another corn dog and headed for the door.

It didn't take her very long to arrive at Sugar and Spice and she wasn't surprised to see Roam's van waiting across the street for her. He had probably already been there when he had called her, she realized, but that didn't matter. So long as he had something she could use, she was willing to give him a little bit of leeway. She waved to him, sure that he was there even if she couldn't see him, and unlocked the front door. As she switched on the lights, she heard the bell over the front door signaling that he had entered.

She started a pot of tea and watched as he set down an enormous plastic box that seemed to be filled to bursting with file folders and papers. It was full enough that she was impressed he had managed to get the cover secured across the top. "That's a lot more than I had expected," she said as she handed him a cup.

"I've been collecting information on demons for over two years now but some of these records are five or more years old. It's amazing that things this dangerous are out there and nobody seems to care." He blew away some of the steam that wafted up from the cup and sniffed. "What flavor is this?"

"I care," Sahara replied as she sat with her own cup. "It's black currant." It was the flavor she had set out for the next day but there was no reason not to start it early. She motioned toward the box. "Mind if I have a look?"

"Sure, dig in," he said as he pushed the box over towards her. "It actually took me a while to dig through all of my research and pull out everything I have on the demons." He took a drink of his tea and smiled wryly. "I'm not very organized, so it's all just kind of jumbled together."

Sahara lifted the top off the box. "I just appreciate your sharing it with me."

Roam took another drink of his tea. "See, that's another thing I've been wondering about. Why are you so interested in demons?"

She looked up to meet his eyes. "Last time we talked, you said that they were pretty dangerous and that there were a lot of them out there. Why wouldn't I want to learn more?"

"We talked about a lot of things; demon activity was just one of them. What makes demons so important to you?"

She shrugged as she pulled out the top stack of paper. "Maybe they just seemed to be more important than the others. I mean, if Vamps and Weres are getting worse, at least they're the threat we know. But demons?" she looked up to meet his eyes. "Nobody seems to know anything about them. Except you."

"That's true." He took another sip of his tea and leaned back, watching as she flipped through the papers. "Been looking around, then?"

She nodded without looking up. "I did a little bit of online searching and went to the library. I wouldn't even know where to look beyond that." He had news reports about the black knights that had been tormenting the town since the Festival of Souls but Sahara already knew about those. Not only was Jen's team the one that had responded to their arrival during the Festival, Joel had even encountered a pair of them when the team was en route to the demon's house. She set those papers aside and pulled out another stack. If she really needed more information about those things, she could easily ask Troy.

"Yeah, that's the tough part," he agreed. "But the information's out there, if you just know where to look for it."

"So where do you look for stuff like this?" She took another drink of her tea and looked over at him. "When you think there's something out there, how do you find out more? Or is it just by following people around?"

He laughed at that. "Believe it or not, people are not high priority for me. I tend to follow news about everything else but I follow people when I think there's something going on."

"But what about these?" she asked as she held up a few pages of handwritten notes. They appeared to be people that he had been keeping track of, believing that they were possessed by demons of some variety. "These are still people, aren't they?"

"Sort of," he agreed. "They are people but they don't usually act like people." He leaned forward and pulled more notes out of the box. "Like these, for example. They were just like other normal people but for no reason that I have been able to find, they started to act like something else.

"This one," he pointed to one section specifically, "woke up one morning and just decided to kill his family. Wife, kids, all of them, dead. Nobody that isn't being controlled would do something like that."

Sahara wasn't sure she agreed with him on that one. There were a lot of mental illnesses that people suffered from that could have accounted for the strange behavior. When she pointed that out to Roam, however, he just shook his head.

"If it was only one case like that, I might be inclined to believe that too. But three in one month? That's a bit too much to chalk up to coincidence and mental illness."

She took the paper he held out with the news reports and notes he had made about the murders. "Three of them?"

"They weren't all right here but they were all in the northwest and they all used knives to do the killings. All of them woke up early in the morning and killed everyone in the house as they slept. This one," he pointed to another page, "even killed the daughter's boyfriend, who had snuck in for the night. Schizophrenia, or whatever else you want to say it could be, doesn't account for that many similarities."

As Sahara read through the newspaper clippings and his carefully detailed notes, she had to admit she was impressed. She had heard about one of the murders on the news but the other two were new to her. She spent a little while digging through the files he had on the people he believed to be possessed before setting them aside as well. While interesting, possession wasn't what she was looking for. At least, not possession in this manner.

The next stack she picked up was a news report of a serial rapist from a number of years ago who had used an insanity defense at his trial, claiming that he had been controlled by tiny demons that lived in his head. The demons had committed the rapes, he claimed, not him. She could understand why Roam had kept a copy of that report but even the most untrained person could easily see that it was nothing more than a transparent attempt to keep the rapist out of prison.

"What about the female demon you were telling me about?" Sahara asked, trying not to sound overly eager. "I wouldn't think they were very common."

He looked over at her in surprise. "You can't be serious."

"What?" she looked up from the box, surprised at his reaction.

"Demons come in all shapes and sizes. Why wouldn't there be female demons?"

She thought about it for a moment, and then shrugged. "I guess I just never thought about it before." She hadn't, really. Until Jen had been kidnapped, the thought of demons – male or female – had never crossed Sahara's mind.

He nodded and a thin smile curved his lips. "Most people don't. They just assume that all demons are either male or genderless because those are the ones you hear about the most often." He leaned forward to dig through the box. "Plus, some of the demons are pretty hideous and don't even look like humans, so people just seem to assume they're male. But the female demons, the ones that look human, those are some of the most dangerous ones out there."

"Why's that?"

He pulled out the file he was looking for and handed it to her. "Well, there're a couple of reasons. First, nobody suspects that a gorgeous woman is going to be a demon. An ugly woman, maybe, but even then, she's more likely to be labeled a witch than a demon. Big mistake, that."

"Is this the one you met?" she asked as she took the file. When he nodded, she opened the file and began to look through the stack of papers enclosed within. She had to agree with his assessment that a pretty woman would be less suspicious than a plain one, there was a definite assumption of innocence based on how a person appeared, regardless of that person's actual mindset and actions. "So what's the other reason that a demoness would be more dangerous?"

"Because of all the varieties of demons that I've catalogued over the last couple of years, the most likely type of demoness to be found in our world is a succubus."

She looked up at him in surprise again. "Succubus? I thought those were just myths."

He laughed at that, and his eyes lit up with the humor he obviously found in her question. "Not too long ago, werewolves and vampires were just myths, too. You have to realize; most myths are based in fact and legends come from actual events that happened when people weren't ready to deal with the truth of what they were seeing." His explanation sounded rehearsed, as though he had explained the same thing to plenty of people already.

Wondering how many others had completely bought into his theories, Sahara blinked at him. Again, he made a lot of sense. She could completely understand why people would feel scared by the threats he said were out in the world. Personally, Sahara didn't buy into most of it but there was just too much he said that rang true with everything else she had already uncovered.

"But what would make a succubus so dangerous? Don't they just try to sleep with everyone, or try to get everyone to sleep with each other, something like that?"

"Oh, it's much worse than that. For one, they're sadistic little bitches, and so are the males." He gave her a knowing look and went back to digging through the box. "In fact, I'm really not sure which of the two is worse."

"There are males, too? I thought all succubusses were female."

"They are," he said without looking up. "And its succubi, not succubusses. But the males, they're called incubi. Those ones are every bit as bad as the women."

"Okay, so what's so bad about them?" She barely even looked at the file of papers in her hand. What he had to say already scared her enough.

"They're the demonic equivalent of a sexual predator. Where most demons get their energy and power from the dark plane itself, these have to steal it from humans." He glanced up and, noticing the look of horror on her face, quickly pointed out, "Don't worry; a succubus wouldn't generally go after a woman, not unless there wasn't a man nearby to satisfy her. Their mental tricks don't work on women, either."

"That's a relief," Sahara said, although she

didn't feel very relieved at all. The more he explained, the more it sounded like the demon that had taken Jen had been one of these.

"What you should be worried about is that most succubi travel with an incubus. I haven't found one of those in the area, though, but what I understand, there's never one without the other. All of the other demons I've catalogued, they can be out on their own. Sure, there are some that seem to prefer to travel with specific others but for succubi and incubi, it's different. It's as though each needs the other to function for some reason." He looked thoughtful for a moment. "Unless she did have an incubus that she was allied with; he might turn up at some point."

"What happens then?"

He shrugged. "The end of life as we know it. Like I said, they get their power from people and there's almost limitless supply of those out here. Cities are getting larger and more populated, so there's ample food supply for them."

"Food?" she looked over at him in shock. "They eat people?"

He shook his head. "Not in the way you

think. Demons don't eat, so they survive off the energy they take from people." He handed her another news clipping, this one of a four-teen-year-old boy who went missing five years prior. Sahara barely glanced at it as she took it from him.

"And they get this energy through sex?"

"Mostly, although I'm pretty sure that any kind of sexual tension would work. Energy isn't a physical thing, so I doubt they'd actually have to be directly involved to feed off of it."

She chuckled as she thought about it. "I'm sure there are plenty of people who wouldn't think that was so bad. I mean, most guys would beg for sex, so being required to perform prob-ably wouldn't be that much of a stretch." She thought about it for a moment before adding, "Or even turned on, for that matter."

He shook his head again. "Remember what I said about them being sadistic? It isn't just the sex that feeds them... it's the violence, too. The more violent the act, the more power they gain." His mouth tightened in a fierce scowl. "And the more power they suck out of their victim, the less energy the victim has. They'll drain a person until there's nothing left but an empty, catatonic shell."

Sahara did her best to hide the shiver of fear that started at her hairline and travelled down her spine to her tailbone. She wasn't very successful at it, if the look of sympathy Roam sent her way had anything to say about it.

"Look," he sighed. "I wasn't just taking my time and gathering all this together before I called you today. I had to make sure that you were someone that could be trusted. So I did some checking into you."

"You were spying on me?" She looked up at him in surprise. Given what she already knew about the conspiracy buff, she shouldn't have been surprised but his admission still took her off guard.

He nodded. "And I think I know why you're so interested in demons. One of your friends works for New World Response, doesn't she?" When Sahara agreed, he lowered his head. "I know that New World is the company that responded to the black knights and I think they were out in the same area where I found the succubus.

"Now your friend isn't anywhere to be found, unusual considering how much of the news-paper has been devoted to her lately. Instead, there are lots of people running all over the place, casting magical spells and trying to break into the hospital to talk to a psychic."

He paused for a long moment before contin-uing. "Was she taken by one of them?"

Sahara felt tears well up in her eyes, and quickly stood up to pour each of them another cup of tea. "My reasons are personal and I don't want to talk about it." She stayed with the teapot until she felt like she was back under control. "I just want to find out as much about these demons as I can. If you can help me, I'll work with you. If not, I'll have to look some-where else."

Roam silently accepted the cup she offered him. "I wasn't trying to upset you," he explained gently once she sat down. "I just think it's nice to see that someone cares and her disappear-ance hasn't just gone unnoticed."

"What do you mean?"

He took a drink of the tea and looked up at her. "Do you know how many people go missing every day? Hundreds," he answered before she had a chance to think about it. "Thousands, in some places, places where the population is a lot denser and there wouldn't be as much notice if a handful of them go missing. I'm not saying that all of them are being taken by demons but most of the demons I've come across aren't satisfied with only taking one or two people.

"I was just thinking that when we find your friend, we might find some of the others, too."

Sahara sighed. "I'm just trying to find out what I can. I'm not a mage or a psychic or anything like that, I'm just an herbalist. For the most part, everyone else has had something that they can do to help but I've been stuck here, worrying and feeling useless. This is the only thing that I've found that I can do that might actually help."

"I suspected as much. From what I've been able to tell, you and this Jen woman seem to go pretty far back. If I was in your position and one of my friends had been captured by demons, I'd do everything in my power to get them back, too. But like I told you earlier, I'm willing to help as much as I can." He wryly gestured at the accumulated research he had brought with him. "That's why I brought so much more than just what you were asking about."

"I appreciate that," Sahara smiled wanly at him. She considered asking him to keep Jen's predicament a secret but she doubted that there would be much point in doing so. Roam seemed to sympathize with her and, as much of a pain he had been to Bobby and some of the others in town, he didn't seem to be truly malicious. Beyond that, she realized even as she felt like a heel for her latest train of thought, even if he did end up telling someone about why he was in her shop that night, she doubted that anyone would believe him. That was the catch to being a conspiracy theorist like he was, she guessed. Even when you uncover a truth, people just assume you're crazy.

"So what kind of things are you still looking for?" He motioned towards the box. "There's a lot of stuff there, so if you want to find something in particular, I'll probably have an easier time finding it."

She shrugged. "I believe it but I just don't even know what I'm looking for." She took another sip of her tea. "I guess I was just hoping that you'd have that magical little nugget of information that would tell us how to find her and bring her home." She looked at the box of research. "I think we'll just have to go through everything until something jumps out at us."

Roam thought for a moment, sipping at his own cup and tapping on the handle. "New World responded to the attack in the area I spent some time researching, so if your friend was taken by the same demon I've been track-ing, it would make sense to start on the local information. There isn't a lot of it but what I do have shouldn't be too hard to find.

"I'm guessing you already know about the house I found, since that seems to be where she disappeared from." When Sahara agreed, he looked thoughtful again. "I know that these types of demons usually hang out at sexually charged places, like orgies and stuff like that." He wiggled his eyebrows at her. "We could give it a try."

Sahara shot him a look of incredulity. "You can't be serious."

"About the types of places where the demons

hang out? Yeah, I am. About us having an orgy? Not really. But if we can think of a place with a lot of sexual energy, it's fairly likely we'll be able to find either a succubus or an incubus there." He took another drink. "If there even is one still in town. Like I said, the one I knew about hasn't been around for a little while now. She may have moved on to another area."

She wasn't sure she believed him or not but considering that was where they got their power, it made some sense. "Would a stripper bar work?" She didn't spend much of her daily life pondering the existence and locations of all the strip joints in town but she knew that there were at least a couple. Maybe even more, she wasn't sure. Either way, she shouldn't have too difficult of a time finding out. If she remembered correctly, one of her friends had taken her resident ghost to one recently as a reward for good behavior at Collin's birthday party.

He thought for only a moment before nodding. "Yeah, that's a pretty sexual place. I wouldn't be surprised if they were regulars in places like that." He grinned over at her. "You need an escort? I'd be happy to go with you."

"A friend of mine went out to a place not too long ago; she said it wasn't too bad. I'll have to call her and find out where it was so I can have a look." She looked over at Roam again. "So how can you tell if there's a succubus or an incubus there?" She had no idea how to spot one in a crowd. From all that she had been told and from the badly-scribbled notes she was reading, the succubus he had been tracking seemed to look just like regular person.

"Well, it'd be simpler if you had psychic talent. That would make it easier to sense things like demons." He thought for a moment. "Lacking that, I guess I'd be looking for the most attractive ones, for starters. Both of them need to be pretty damn sexy to attract the energy they need." He took another drink of his tea. "They probably wouldn't be in a group or, if they are, it'd be one male with a bunch of women, or vice versa."

Sahara nodded, taking another sip of her tea. "Then I guess I just need to find a way to keep from falling under its spell while I'm there."

He looked up at her in surprise. "You're planning to go yourself?" he set his cup down and leaned towards her. "I thought you were going to pass the information to someone else and have them go in after the demons. Someone like New World or another of the response teams here in town."

"I'm not sure what I'm going to do with all this yet," she replied. "What about a ghost or a poltergeist? Would either of them be able to sense a demon?"

"Probably, but both of those make for pretty unreliable backup. You need to call in a response team if you're planning something like tracking down a demon."

She waved him off. "I know of both; one is the most reliable person I know and the other's got no choice." She checked her watch and discovered it was still early enough to try. "I need to make some calls."

"You're going now?" he asked in amazement.

She nodded as she pulled out her phone and dialed a number from memory. "Hey, Angie, remember that bar you took Eric to after Collin's birthday party? Do you think you guys could meet me there?"

Chapter 8

Thick, black mists swirled around the clearing. There was no wind, no air movement to cause the mist to shift as it did but still the shadows billowed and flowed. Shapes would occasionally appear in the darkness, human faces alongside shapes that were clearly not human, fading away to nothingness as quickly as they appeared. Shadows added to shadows, making visibility almost nil but up ahead in the distance, almost out of visual range, glowed a faint blue light.

Steve Jenkins stepped into the swirling darkness, clenching his fists against the fear. For far too long he had been trapped in its dense mass, held prisoner and unable to escape. Now, he faced the mists again, but this time was different.

This time, he wasn't the one who was trapped inside.

The haze closed in around him as he stepped further into its depths, taking one cautious step after another and looking around at the myriad of faces that briefly appeared before fading away into nothingness again. He knew that if he reached out, the mist would recede from his fingertips but wouldn't completely go away, leaving faint impressions where he had moved it. Drawing shapes and designs in the fog had been one of the few entertainments afforded him while he had been imprisoned in this awful place. Now he wondered why he had been called here again.

He wasn't trapped, deep inside he could tell the difference, but someone was.

The blue light became brighter as he approached and he wondered if he shone as brightly as whoever had called him. When he finally got close enough to discover who it was, he stopped in shock.

A battered woman sat on the ground, the

tattered remnants of clothing all that covered her nudity but for the shackles and chains that held her in place. Her back was covered in welts, as were her arms and legs. Fresh bruises colored her skin with angry purple and blue splotches, a mosaic of pain. He didn't immediately recognize her but something about the injured woman seemed familiar. Even when she looked up and met his eyes, it took a moment for his brain to register who she was.

"Jen?"

She blinked as though she could only barely see him, and he wondered how extensive the damage was. Finally, her eyes widened in recognition. "You came," she breathed.

"Of course I came," he said as he tried to walk to her side. An invisible barrier blocked him from reaching her, the cage with which he was so well acquainted, and he had to stop just outside of arm's reach. "What happened to you?"

"You were right," she explained. "The demon had traps that I hadn't expected." She shrugged one bloody shoulder in resigned acceptance of her fate. "I got caught up in one." Before she had gone with her team to try and capture the demon that had instead trapped her, the dreamwalker had warned her to be careful and wary of the demon's traps. Jen had thought she was prepared but recent circumstances had convinced her otherwise.

"What about your friends? Are they there with you?" Though he couldn't see anyone else with her, that didn't mean that she was alone. The last time he had seen Jen, she had been working with an entire crowd of people.

She shook her head. "No. I don't know what happened to any of them. Last time I saw them, they were being held by the demon in her house." She explained about the mind control that the demoness had exerted over her team, how she had forced them to hand her over to another demon. "I don't know how she did it," Jen said.

The dreamwalker nodded. "The demons have different abilities, so it doesn't surprise me that one would turn up with something like that." He stood up and paced back and forth, just outside the unseen barrier. "You're glowing a lot more than I remember. After we finish here,

I will check on your team and see if they are captives as well or if they managed to escape."

She shook her head. "I doubt they got away but I appreciate your checking in on them for me."

As he walked, he trailed a couple fingers across the transparent wall. After he made a complete circuit, he sighed. The cage was every bit as impregnable from the outside as he remembered it to be on the inside. "I don't know how to get in to you. The wall's like glass."

"I think I'm stuck pretty well," Jen admitted. "I've been looking but there's no way out. The chains don't have any give and I can't pull the hooks out of the wall." She reached up and touched the collar. "I can't even get this stupid thing off." She looked up at him in confusion. "What do you mean, I'm glowing?" She looked down at her hands, and then at her legs, before meeting his eyes again. "I'm not glowing."

"You're only stuck because you're only using your hands," he explained to her. "If the demons are holding you in Derathim, there isn't anything solid there. It's all illusions. Try using your energy, instead." As she tried to speak, he held up a hand. "I know it all seems real." He looked around the misty walls that still flowed around them and shuddered. "Believe me, I know how real it feels but none of it is. It's just the dark energy that's trying to block your normal power." He just hoped that she was strong enough to block out enough of the dark energy to not end up tainted with it like he had been.

"But I don't have any power," she interrupted.

"I know," he said. "But you need to block out the dark energy, it's keeping you from getting to your own." He looked at her speculatively. "But then, if you couldn't get to your power, you shouldn't be glowing so much."

Jen sighed. "Okay, what's with the glowing? What are you talking about?"

He looked down at her, trying to decide if she was kidding. Finally, he decided that she might not realize how much light she was putting off. "Your energy beacon, that's how I found you. Didn't you realize it was on?"

"I have no idea what you're talking about."

How could she not know? He wondered to himself. "It's one of the first things I was told after my testing was over, to keep an eye on my beacon and the beacons of others. Didn't they tell you about that?" It seemed like standard protocol, as far as he could remember. Every other psychic he had spoken with had similar experiences after their testing.

Jen shook her head. "I'm guessing you're talking about your psychic testing. The only thing I was told at the end of mine was that I had almost as much power as a block of cheese."

His eyes widened at her statement. "You've got to be kidding; what kind of idiot tested you?" When she simply blinked in response, he explained. "People glow when they have power; it's one of the easiest ways to determine a person's power level. The stronger they are, the brighter they glow."

"And I'm glowing?" her face was twisted with confusion.

"Brightly. I think you might be glowing more than I do." He looked at the amount of power that shone in her beacon. He couldn't quite tell but it seemed to be flickering slightly. He hadn't ever seen that particular effect in a beacon before and he made a mental note to find out what it meant.

"But I can't manipulate energy the way other people can."

"If the people who tested you didn't think you had any power, then you weren't ever trained, were you?" When she shook her head, he nodded. "That would be why. Using energy isn't easy." No wonder she was flickering so much. That much energy output couldn't be easy to maintain, especially without proper training. On the other hand, if that was her natural energy output, he had to wonder how immense it must be when she learned how to focus and direct it.

She looked thoughtful for a moment but then shook it off. "Any way you look at it, it doesn't matter right now. I have to find a way to get out of here, so I need to find out where *here* is. Can you help me?"

"I'm not really sure. I can't come there, not physically and not dreamwalking either. Even if I could walk there, it wouldn't do any good be-cause I can't manifest when I'm out and about." He thought for a moment. "But I think I might know of a way that will help others to be able to find you.

"You see," he explained, "Derathim is masked from our world by the energy that sustains it. The energy itself comes from the heart of the dark plane, so there isn't anything we can do about that. However, if we can make you brighter, it will be easier for you to be seen when people are looking for you."

"Make me brighter? What does that mean?"

"Remember what I said about your beacon? If you can draw in enough energy, that will make your glow extend further out. The more power a person is either holding or using, the brighter they become. That means that if we can maximize the amount of power you contain, it will make you like a lighthouse in the sea of darkness."

Jen nodded slowly as he spoke. "Like a tracking beacon. That way Todd, or whoever else is looking for me, will have an idea on where to look." This was more than she could have hoped for. If anyone could find her, Todd could. For her to be sending out a tracking beacon like the dreamwalker was talking about would just make it that much easier for him to do so.

He grinned. "Exactly. So the more energy you are able to draw in, the easier it will be for them to find you. And I, for my part, will inform others of how you can be found."

"You're a genius, you know that?" she smiled at him.

"The hard part is going to remain with you, I'm afraid. If you are in Derathim, there isn't much there besides dark energy, which is highly dangerous to use. Unfortunately, there aren't many other options because learning how to absorb only one type of energy and not another will take some time to teach you, time we don't have. We will simply have to deal with the repercussions of dark exposure taint once you are returned to us."

"You're saying that it's going to suck pretty badly when I get home. Not much difference there." She looked up at him. "So how do I draw in the energy?"

They spent the better part of an hour with him explaining how to draw in the energy and her trying to mimic what he was telling her.

As they worked, he noticed that her bruises and welts had started to heal. The marks faded until he could barely see where they had been. By the time they finished, the only traces of her injuries were the smears of dried blood. Was it something to do with the dark energy, he wondered, or were they simply a manifestation of her feeling captured? He hadn't ever seen anything like that before but Jen in and of herself wasn't like anything he had ever seen before. He had already discovered that underestimating this woman, or even expecting her to behave in the same manner as others would, was a mistake.

When he noticed her beacon getting brighter, he told her, so that she would know she was doing it right. Finally, when she was able to flare her beacon almost twice as brightly as it had been when he arrived, he decided she had gotten the hang of it. "Just keep doing that and they'll have no trouble finding you."

She grinned at him, and he smiled back, hoping that he hadn't done something awful to her. If she became too enmeshed in the energies that he had taught her to absorb, he had no idea what would happen to her. At the very least, he recognized that she was in better physical condition than she had been an hour ago, assuming that her visual aspect with which he had been interacting reflected her physical form. If not, then he could take solace in the idea that her mental state had improved. That wasn't much consolation but it was better than nothing.

"I have to go soon," she explained once he pronounced her ready. "If I'm not awake, the demons'll take someone else and I'd rather they not do that."

He lowered his eyes and nodded, under-standing immediately where the marks had come from, and why. "Don't go too overboard," he cautioned her. "You of all people know what they're capable of."

She smiled up at him, but it was a tired, weary smile. "I know. But I have to do this."

"I know. Be strong; we'll be there for you soon."

"I sure hope so," her voice lingered even as she faded from view. "Because this place sucks."

The swirling mists closed in around him and

stopped moving. Seconds later, he was alone in a black, empty space. He could hear voices and, as he listened, he started to recognize words.

"I don't know; he's been like this for a couple hours now." A female voice spoke, sounding stressed and confused.

"Has this happened before?" Another voice, this one male, responded to the woman.

"A couple of times but never for this long."

There was a rustling sound, like papers being shuffled, and a bright light flared into the darkness. "Where's the on-staff psychic?" the male voice asked. "Shouldn't he be here by now?"

"There's no reason to shout," Steve explained as he looked back and forth between the nurse and the doctor. "I can hear you just fine, you know."

The woman, who was dressed in a nurse's uniform, dropped the printout that she had been flipping through. "Mr. Jenkins! You're awake!" She rushed forward to have a closer look.

"Of course I'm awake, how's anyone supposed to sleep with the two of you arguing over me like that?" he asked but there was no anger behind his words. He looked over to the doctor, who was looking at him, dumbfounded, and gestured for him to come closer. "I need a cup of coffee, a change of clothes, and a phone, immediately." He needed to make a phone call before he forgot the number that Jen had given him.

He smiled to himself as he remembered the expression on her face as she told him, "This time, you get to be the one calling in the middle of the night."

Chapter 9

Shadows stretched across the walls, deepening with every hour that Todd sat at the table reading the same page of information and whispering quietly to himself. He had been running through the complex planar travel spell for three days and still wasn't positive that he had the pronunciation right on a couple of the terms. He knew that this spell was the last option he could offer to find his sister, if only he could get it right.

He pushed the book away and yawned, stretching his arms high over his head to straighten his back out. He hadn't been to see his chiropractor in over a month and his body didn't appreciate the oversight. As he turned his head to stretch his neck, he noticed that the clock on the stove said it was after three in the morning. "No, that can't be right," he said to himself as he checked his watch. "Damn, I've been here longer than I thought; no wonder I'm sore." He glanced at the plate and fork that still sat on the table, pushed a few inches away from his spell book. It still held the remnants of the midnight snack Mary had made for him before she and Jaime had gone back to their hotel for the night.

He stood up and stretched again before putting the dishes into the sink and closing his spell book. Staying up any later wouldn't do him or his sister any good. In the living room, Patrick was asleep on the new couch and Troy was curled up in his recliner, which Patrick had dubbed the Bark-O-Lounger. Its title was even emblazoned on the side of the chair in black spray paint, slightly burned from a recent house fire. The spell of silence that Todd had placed over the two of them would be wearing off soon and Todd wanted to be asleep before their snores made that activity impossible.

Rather than heading all the way out to his hotel and having to turn around and come back to the house again first thing in the morning, he decided to use Jen's bed. He had to admit to himself as he crawled under the covers that just being in her room and surrounded by her things made him feel like she was close, almost close enough to reach out and touch.

With any luck, he would get the spell memorized soon, and that would become a reality.

He rolled onto his side and his eyes fell upon a small stuffed teddy bear on the nightstand that he recognized. He had given it to her on their birthday, he wasn't sure how many years ago. He reached out a hand and pulled the bear under the covers next to him. Almost before his eyes completely closed, he was asleep.

When he woke, it was later than he had intended. He stumbled out towards the scent of coffee and discovered Troy and Patrick blocking the kitchen door, deep in conversation. "What's going on?"

Troy looked down at Todd and stepped out of the way. "Bad news. William wasn't able to reach the dreamwalker like we'd hoped."

Todd poured a cup of coffee. "Well, we knew it was a long shot. Besides, even if William had managed to talk with him, there wasn't any guarantee that he'd be able to reach Jen."

"That's what I was trying to say," Patrick agreed. "But at least we have something to go on, since your spell is going to be able to find her." He looked over at his brother. "Right?"

"As long as I can get the spell to work right, it should go directly to her." He took a drink of the lukewarm coffee and wondered how long ago it had been brewed. For right that moment, it didn't matter but he dumped out the rest of the pot and started a new one. Just because Troy didn't mind drinking day-old coffee, that didn't mean that he had to suffer the same fate. "I'm just having a little more difficulty than I thought with getting the spell down," he admitted.

"Is there anything we can do to help?" Patrick asked.

"Not really." Todd leaned against the counter and took another drink of his coffee. "It's just a really hard spell and I haven't ever used it before. I want to get it right." He didn't want to worry them by explaining exactly how badly things might go if he got it wrong.

Troy looked at him thoughtfully. "Are you sure you can do this?"

"It's just taking a bit longer than I'd expected." He turned towards the fridge. "Is there anything in here for breakfast, or have you two eaten it all already?"

"He ate it," both of them said in unison, pointing at each other.

"No big deal," Todd sighed. On a hunch, he opened the freezer and pulled out a box of blueberry toaster waffles. He looked at the box for a long moment before pulling out the last pair of frozen discs. "Remind me to pick up more of these later today, would you?"

Patrick looked at his watch. "I really should be at the site by now." He looked over at Todd. "Unless I should stay home." The hopeful expression he wore explained more than words could what he was truly asking. The only reason that Todd would suggest Patrick stay home from work would be that Todd was ready to cast the spell.

Todd shook his head. "No, you go to work. I doubt I'll have much of a breakthrough before you get back." He popped the waffles into the toaster. "And if by some miracle I do make that breakthrough while you're gone, I doubt I'll be the first to call you."

Patrick nodded and headed out. "I'll be back around seven or so," he called over his shoulder as he walked out the door. "But seriously, if you find anything, if you need anything, let me know."

Once the door was closed, Troy reached up into a cupboard and pulled out the syrup for Todd. "So how dangerous is this, really?"

Todd half shrugged. "Probably more than just a basic illusion but there are far worse spells, I'm sure."

"But how badly is this going to mess you up?" Troy looked at him. "Physically, mentally, any of it. What's it going to do?"

"Where are Mary and Jaime?"

"Shopping. There isn't anyone here to overhear this conversation."

Todd pulled his waffles out of the toaster. "Honestly, I have no idea what it's going to do; like I said, I've never used it before."

"Okay, worst-case scenario?"

Todd shrugged. "I'm not worried about what

happens to me. I just want to get Jen back." He slathered butter across his waffles before pouring the syrup over them. "Besides, that isn't really what I'm worried about."

"Afraid the NPIB's going to find out about it?" Troy asked as he put the syrup away.

Todd shook his head. "The NPIB isn't the all-powerful entity that everyone believes they are."

"Then who are you sacred of?" Troy asked.

"You know how it goes, no matter what species, breed, or anything you are, there's a hierarchy. In the military you have rank, in business, you have supervisors, in breed, you have lineage." He took another bite. "With mages, psychics, all of that, there are plenty of more powerful people above you that want to stay there."

"And there isn't much worse than a bunch of grouchy old mages with too much power." Troy nodded. "And you're worried that they'll find out what you're up to?"

He took a bite and looked over at Troy. "I'm not supposed to be using this spell."

Troy blinked at him in surprise. "Why not?"

"I have it but it's for research only. I'm not allowed to cast it." He took another bite.

"And that would make you as powerful as one of them, wouldn't it?"

Todd took another bite of his waffle. "They like their power and they don't like to share."

"So we need to keep them from finding out what we're up to."

Todd took another drink of his coffee. "I've only spoken to one person about all this. I've known him for years and I trust him but even so I didn't tell him much."

"Fine," Troy responded. "You just worry about getting Jen back and I'll take care of the rest."

"I hate to burst your bubble," Todd said as he eyed Troy, "but you're just a hybrid."

"Maybe so, but I have a few tricks up my sleeves and a few years of practice."

"You have a few years. They have a few hundred." He drained the last of his coffee. "The Venerali Magii don't become so powerful overnight, you know." He glanced at Troy. "And you are mortal, whether you want to believe it or not."

Troy looked over at the coffeepot. The light was still on, so it was still brewing. "You weren't surprised."

"At what?" Todd blinked at him in confusion, wondering whether he had missed a portion of the conversation. "Surprised about what?"

"Me. The first time you came out to visit Jen after I moved in, it's like you knew I was here."

"I did know you were here. Jen's my sister and I tend to watch out for her." He looked over at the hybrid. "And if I'd thought you were up to no good, you wouldn't be here now."

"Right, you mages have that far-seeing thing going on."

"Yep, I'm a regular peeping Todd." The knife in his stomach twisted again as he remembered how often Jen had used that phrase.

When the front door opened, he changed the subject. "Since this is a travel spell, I'm assuming you want to go? You realize that we have no idea what's going to be on the other side when the portal opens."

"Hell, yes. I'm going." The light went out on the coffee maker and both men moved for the pot. "And I don't particularly care what wants to get in my way."

Even as tired as he still was, Todd was slightly faster. He poured himself a cup before handing the pot over to Troy. "I have a limit on how many people I can bring with me. I have to go, obviously, to keep the door open. You'll make two."

"And we make four," Jaime added as she and Mary stepped into the kitchen. "When are we going?"

Todd shook his head. "You aren't going," he said.

"Why not?" Jaime demanded. "She's our sister, too."

"I know and that's why you aren't going. I need someone I trust to stay here and help us get her back out once we get inside." He wrapped an arm around his big sister. "But we're not ready yet, anyway."

Jaime tried to protest, but Troy interrupted. "Your sister's been held captive by a demon and for quite a while. She's going to need someone she immediately recognizes and knows that she can trust waiting for her when we bring her out." He pointed at Todd. "The only reason he's going instead of waiting with you guys is because he's got the magic. What she needs on the other side is people with guns and lots of ammo."

Jaime scowled at the hybrid. "Okay, I get that she needs familiar people when you bring her out. But don't you dare talk down to me about what you think I can and can't do." She reached into her purse and pulled out a pistol that was almost the same size as Troy's favorite handgun. "I live alone, in the downtown district of one of the largest and most dangerous cities in the world. You thought I didn't have a gun?"

Troy raised his eyebrows. "But how well can you use it?"

"Probably better than you can," she retorted as she put the weapon back into her purse. "My instructor was a retired sniper and I take a refresher course every six months."

Todd reached out and poked at her purse. "What I'm wondering," he mused, "Is how you fit that huge gun into this little purse."

"That's easy," she explained. "You have your magic and I have mine." She winked at her brother, pulled a bottle of water out of the fridge and headed back out to the living room.

Once she was gone, Todd looked over at Troy. "She's not kidding, you know."

"About what?" he asked as he took another drink of his coffee.

"When she first moved out to go to college, dad insisted that she take self-defense classes. She kept up with them even after she left, and I believe she's running a couple of self-defense courses at her company, too."

"It's dangerous to be a woman out on your own like that."

"That's what he thought too." Todd took another drink of his coffee. "After that, it turned into this strange family tradition."

"Everybody gets self-defense classes before leaving the nest?" Troy asked thoughtfully. "Sounds like a strange tradition but it makes a bit of sense beneath it all."

Todd shrugged. "Jen skipped out on it but that was her decision. You know Jen; she's always been kind of headstrong." He took another drink of his coffee. "I should get back to my spell."

"Do you need help with anything?" Troy asked as Todd headed back towards the bedroom.

Todd shook his head, but then he stopped and turned back to Troy. "How many people do you think are going to want to be going on this? Like I said earlier, the spell only lets a certain number of people through the doorway, so I should probably have an idea of how many people are planning to go."

"I'll talk to everyone and see what they have to say. Is there a cap?"

"Yeah," Todd nodded. "I think I can probably safely take ten people, including me, but that'll be about it. Any more than that goes into the iffy zone."

"Okay. I'll see what I can do. We'll try to keep it under ten."

When he got back to the bedroom, Todd checked on his supplies. Most of his magical equipment was still in the living room where he had moved it to after affirming that Jen was alive but there were some things that he just needed peace and quiet for, things like studying the spell itself, so he had moved a few things back into Jen's bedroom. Everything was still as he had left it the night before so setting up to get started again took almost no time.

Although most people believed that spell casting was fairly easy, just a matter of pointing your fingers and chanting in some sort of arcane language, in reality it was much more difficult than that. It didn't take much to cast a simple spell but in order to maintain a more difficult spell the caster had to have a clear understanding of the mechanics behind it. What Todd had spent so much time studying wasn't the spell itself but was instead the underlying parts that allowed the spell to work.

Since he didn't have much experience casting planar spells, it had been a lot more difficult to decipher than a standard travelling spell. However, his extensive knowledge behind the use of travelling spells and the research he had been conducting on the planar spell had finally given him the breakthrough on how a planar travel spell worked. By the time Patrick got home that evening, Todd was reasonably certain that he had figured out how he could make it happen. As far as the pronunciation of the terms he was unfamiliar with, a quick phone call to Chris had helped enormously.

"I think I've got it," he explained to the group in the living room when he finally emerged. "I just need to pick up a few more supplies but I should be ready to cast by tomorrow night." Mary and Jaime had spent days gathering the list of components that he had sent them after but there were still a few things that were either difficult to find or needed to be cut or formed to exacting specifications. Much as he trusted his sisters, Todd didn't want to take any chances.

Everyone started to whoop and holler at his announcement. Almost in unison, Mary and Jaime jumped to their feet and ran over to hug him. The pair of women almost knocked him over in their excitement and Todd would have tumbled to the floor had they not been on opposite sides of him. Even Patrick had to walk over and clap him on the back, making Todd's already sore shoulders even more so. He wasn't about to complain about a little bit of ache, however, not when they were so close to retrieving his sister.

At the other end of the room, Troy's face broke into a wide grin as he watched the celebrating family. Folding his arms across his chest, he leaned against the wall and watched.

Once everyone let go, Todd looked over at Troy. "Have you talked to them yet?"

"Patrick and I are going and the ladies will stay here to help Jen when we bring her back, like we talked about earlier. I talked to Joel earlier, too and he wants to help also."

Patrick nodded his agreement. "I think we should bring Jen's team in on this, too. Even if they can't go through the mirror with us to get her, they can be here for when we all get back."

"Sounds like a plan," Todd answered and turned to Troy to ask, "How many people did you say there are on her team?"

"Four others," Troy supplied. "Marc, Ty, J.J., and Mike."

"I'll call them now." Patrick pulled out his phone and dialed.

Todd tallied the volunteers on his fingers. "That would make eight, so we can do that. When we get Jen, that'll make nine, which is still inside the limit.

"I guess we can spend the rest of tonight getting ready, then." Todd stepped into his sneakers. "I still need to go out and pick up a few components, so I'll be back soon."

Before Todd had a chance to head out, Patrick signaled him to wait. "Okay, I'll let them know," he said as he hung up the phone. "David thinks we should cast this at the office so if anything happens, it won't destroy the house again."

"Makes sense," Troy agreed. "After all, you just got the front wall fixed from the last time."

"Also, David said he heard from the dreamwalker. He talked to Jen and confirmed that she's alive, at least. He said she's trying to find a way out, too, but she's in Derathim somewhere and there aren't a lot of exits out of there."

He looked over at Todd. "He wanted me to let you know to look for her beacon. He said you'd know what it meant."

Todd nodded slowly. "I do but it doesn't make any sense. A beacon's a signal that a mage or a psychic puts out, showing their power level," he explained as he looked around the group.

"Jen doesn't have a power level though, so how could she have a beacon?"

"Is there any way to put one of those beacons on someone else?" Mary offered. "You had said that the dreamwalker's a psychic, didn't you? Maybe we need to look for his beacon on her."

Todd hadn't ever heard of anyone having the ability to artificially place a beacon on another person but he wasn't a specialist in psychic abilities so there was a chance he just hadn't heard about it. "I guess it's possible but it doesn't really matter. We know where she's at so we don't need to look for a beacon, his or hers, to find her."

"Either way," he stepped closer to the door, "it's good that he was able to talk with her and verify she's more or less okay. That's a relief, in and of itself. Now we just need to go get her, so I need to go get those components."

Chapter 10

When David Melrose arrived at the office the next afternoon, he was in a better mood than he had been in for well over two weeks. The town was covered in a light dusting of snow and more flakes continued to fall even as he parked in his reserved spot and walked into the New World Response office. As usual, he was the first to arrive, so he turned on the lights and started the coffeepot. At least the heater in the building continued running on low power overnight so the interior wasn't quite as bone-numbingly cold as the exterior.

Once the coffee finished brewing, he poured himself a cup and headed downstairs to make sure there was enough room in the basement for Todd to use his magic. He wasn't sure how much space the mage would need but he figured that he would estimate high. If his best guess still didn't provide enough room for him to work, there would be plenty of people there to help him rearrange stuff.

When he decided that he finally had enough open space and, just as importantly, that he needed more coffee, he headed back to the elevator. It felt good to actually be doing things again instead of just sitting at his desk and assigning tasks to other people. There was nothing more frustrating than the helpless feeling of knowing there wasn't a damned thing you could do about a situation but sit behind a desk and try to manage the aftermath. As the elevator slowly crept up to his third-floor office, he allowed himself to hope that Jen wouldn't be too damaged when they got her back.

Given the circumstances, he knew that asking for her to be returned safe and healthy was a bit too much to expect. With everything that she had been through, her just being alive was a reasonable goal.

He looked at the clock and realized that he only had about an hour to get into his paperwork before Charlie Winters showed up for his morning briefing, so if he was going to get any work done without the NPIB staff analyst breathing down his neck and watching his every move, he needed to get to it soon. But Charlie soon enough stepped into David's office, had a seat, and set his own cup of morning beverage on the desk in front of him.

"It doesn't look like your team's been coming up with very much towards finding Ms. Rice. Because of that, my office has decided to bring in a team of their own, which should start to show more results." If nothing else, the man could get directly to the point, a quality which normally David appreciated but the news he delivered was anything but welcome.

The NPIB officer had spent the last few days since his arrival going back and forth between David's office to meet with him and downstairs to meet with the team and had, in David's opinion, accomplished very little. Now it appeared that he had been doing a bit more behind the scenes than David had been aware of. For the NPIB to decide to bring in their own team was no shock, he was just surprised that Charlie was admitting it this readily. "When will they be arriving?"

"Tomorrow evening, at the latest. I know that you had wanted to keep this in-house as much as possible but, to be honest, it has already been far too long."

"I can understand your position on that. However, there have been a couple of new developments that I was only recently made aware of. The way things are looking right now, your team just might end up getting here too late as well."

"What does that mean?" Charlie asked as he leaned forward to pick his cup back off the desk. He took a drink and looked at David, curious. "What new developments?"

"You aren't the only one that's been trying to find her," David explained, taking a drink of his own coffee. "Her brother's been making some pretty impressive progress."

"Todd, right?" when David nodded, he smiled. "I've heard some pretty impressive stuff about that kid. Seems to be a decent mage, from the reports I've received on him." He took another sip of his drink and set the cup down again.

"But you need to realize that, talented as Todd may be, he doesn't have that much experience as a mage and even less in planar kidnapping. The team that's coming in will be bringing in one of the Venerali Magii, someone who does have the experience we need."

"Like I said, it might be for nothing." He leveled his gaze at Charlie over the rim of his coffee cup. "Todd's already found her." Though he knew that the sensation would be short-lived, David took immense pleasure in having the upper hand for once. Charlie had already admitted that his people didn't have the slightest clue about Jen's whereabouts and now he had expressed his doubts on Todd's capabilities. The fact that the people in whom the NPIB so clearly lacked faith had managed to accomplish what Charlie implied they couldn't was immensely gratifying.

Charlie blinked at him in shock. "He has? When did this happen? I hadn't been informed."

"That's because it only happened last night. They're planning to bring her back today."

Charlie shook his head. "From my understanding, Todd can't perform a planar travel spell. How are they going to get there?"

"They've enlisted a little more help than you might know about. It isn't just Jen's family and my team that have been working on this. They've enlisted help from the dreamwalker as well and he's already been in contact with her."

"Jenkins? I thought he was still comatose, how was he able to talk with her?"

David shrugged. "Apparently he was doing some travelling while he was in the coma. He woke up and called me to tell me what he had discovered."

"When was this?"

"Not long ago." He chuckled, remembering the strange phone call he had received before three that morning. "I think he enjoyed waking me up while I was sleeping last night. As far as when he'll be released from the hospital, they have no reason to keep him any longer and he's signing himself out as we speak. I believe he's planning to be here this afternoon."

"You've verified she's alive? That's good news." Charlie leaned back and smiled. "So he's going to help with getting her back?"

"I don't know all the details yet but every-one's doing all that they can to assist in her rescue. From what I understand so far, there will be a temporary gate opened between here and where Jen is being held. The team's going to go over to get her and bring her back with them. Once everyone's home, the gate will be destroyed."

"In that case, as long as Ms. Rice is retrieved before the NPIB team arrives, I will let them know that they don't need to bother." He stood up and headed for the door. "I'll talk with you more about this soon."

As soon as Charlie was gone, David picked up the phone and dialed Jen's house. He knew that someone would be there to pick it up and he needed to let them know what Charlie had said. After only a few rings, Troy answered.

"How long before you guys will be ready to do this?" David asked as soon as he recognized the voice. "The NPIB team will be here by to-morrow night and Charlie's already been in to pester me once today." He checked his watch and realized it was already almost ten in the morning. "I'd thought you guys were going to be here by now."

"We're walking out the door now," Troy answered. "Todd had a little trouble getting a couple of ingredients for the spell so we had to go pick up the last pieces this morning."

"Just hurry. We need to get her back before the team gets here with their Venerali Magii."

"They're bringing a Magii?" Troy asked. "That's not good. Todd was talking about them earlier and said he didn't want any of them near this. Are you sure?"

"That's what Charlie said, so I would guess so."

Troy swore, barely loud enough for David to hear on the other end of the line. "Okay, we're on our way, we should be there soon. Is there a place that's ready for us to use?"

"Yes. I cleared out a section of the basement that should be big enough. If it's not, we can move more stuff out of the way to make more room."

"Is the team already there?"

David clicked on his computer and pulled up

the video surveillance of the basement meeting room. "Yep, they're all ready."

"Okay then, we'll see you soon."

As soon as he got off the phone with Troy, David headed down to the basement to meet with his team. Everyone was either nervously or anxiously pacing back and forth across the floor or leaning against a wall but as soon as David stepped inside all of their attention immediately turned towards him. "Are they here?" Marc asked.

David shook his head. "Not yet. I just spoke with Troy and they're on their way. Are you guys sure you're ready for this?"

"Ready or not, here we come," J.J. quipped.

"Yeah," Mike agreed. "She's one of us; we can't just leave her there."

"Fair enough," David nodded. "Just remember, once he starts the spell, no matter what happens, I expect all of you to listen to Todd. I don't know how well this spell's going to work, or for how long, so if he says to back out, you do what he says, got it?"

Everyone nodded in agreement. "Sounds fair to me, too," Charlie said as he walked into the meeting room. "But aren't we missing a few people?"

The gathered group looked over at him in surprise. "What are you doing here?" Ty asked. He didn't move from his spot against the wall but his posture changed, barely perceptibly but apparent to anyone who knew him: he didn't appreciate Charlie's intrusion in the matter. His opinion was shared by other members of the team; as one, they turned to face the newcomer.

"Same as you, I'm going to help bring your team member back." If he was flustered by the combined might of the New World Response team, Charlie didn't show it. Whether it was due to his training or his natural coolness, David couldn't tell but there was no sign of apprehension on the NPIB officer.

Marc shook his head. "No way." He looked between Charlie and David. "He's not coming with us."

"I don't like it any more than you do," Charlie explained, "but my office is pretty insistent on this. I'm the only agent in the area that's available to go with you and they were pretty adamant that you need to have someone from the Board when you go to Derathim."

Marc looked at David as Charlie spoke. "Do we have any say in this?"

"It doesn't look like it." David was even less amused than the rest of them about the idea of Charlie being present when the rest of the group showed up. Todd had already expressed his reservations many times about having a member of the NPIB snooping around while they worked. He wasn't sure how much worse the mage would react to the idea of bringing Charlie along when they left.

"If he's planning to go with us, then he's not going in that," Todd answered for all of them as he walked into the room. "You have no idea what you're walking into and I doubt that suit's going to impress the demons very much." He set a black duffel bag down on one of the tables and looked around the group. "Where's Joel?"

"He's on his way," Troy grunted as he and Patrick carried the heavy mirror past the door. "Be here in just a couple minutes. Where are we putting this?"

"There's a clear area," David pointed further

into the basement. "There should be more than enough room there." He hadn't realized that a mirror of this magnitude was part of the spell-casting process but he was glad that he had cleared the floor all the way to the wall.

As the rest of the equipment was brought in, Todd continued to evaluate Charlie. "Does any-one have any extra gear that he can borrow?"

"Yeah, there's more in the supply closet," Marc offered doubtfully. "Are you sure about this?"

Todd shrugged. "It'll put me at my spell limit but if he doesn't go, you'll all lose your fund-ing." He looked back at Charlie. "Isn't that how this works?"

"Not by my choice and I wasn't going to threaten anybody over it."

"Maybe not but if your office finds out you didn't go and that it was because they wouldn't let you, they're out of business." He picked up his bag and headed for the door. Before he left the room, however, he looked back over his shoulder at Charlie. His eyes darkened as he added, "No matter what happens from here, you're not taking my sister when we get her back. I don't care who you are or who you work for, she stays here."

He and Jen may have been fraternal twins, thus sharing no more genes and features than either of them did with the rest of their siblings but, for that moment, Todd was a carbon copy of his sister. The ferocity in his expression mimicked perfectly the look that David had seen on Jen's face so many times that it caused his throat to constrict.

"That's not my decision to make and I'm pretty sure you know that."

"I do," Todd answered. "But you'd better let your boss know my position as well." He stepped out the door and turned to catch up with the rest of the group. "She's mine, not yours. You can't have her when she's back."

David looked over at Charlie speculatively. He had watched the interplay between Charlie and Todd and he was surprised at how well it had gone. To be honest, he would have expected Jen's brother to refuse outright to work with Charlie and he wondered why the young man had agreed so easily. Even with the New

World team's funding on the line, David wasn't sure he would have acquiesced so readily.

Even more strangely, Todd hadn't seemed to be the least intimidated by the NPIB agent's presence. "Marc, would you take our friend here to get some proper clothes?"

"Don't worry; I have my own armor and weapons in my car. I'll go get them while you finish getting everything set up."

While Charlie was busily getting ready, David and the rest of the team headed out to see what everyone else was up to. Troy and Patrick had the colossal mirror that they had been carrying set up against one of the walls and Patrick was in the process of securing it in place with thick plastic brackets. Jaime was dragging a small table over next to the mirror, presumably for Todd to put his components onto while he cast the spell. "Are all of you going?" he asked.

Mary looked up at him and shook her head. "Jaime and I are waiting here. The rest of them are going."

"Looks like I'm going to be keeping you ladies company, then," David said. "I'm staying behind, too."

"Keeping an eye on things from this end?" Jaime asked once she had the table in place.

David shook his head. "Nope, I trust my team and your family to do what they need to do. I'm going to have a medical team on standby, though, so if anything happens on the other side, they can put you guys back together again."

Charlie came into the work area dressed in black tactical gear with red patches, the NPIB's Special Forces uniform. He had a pistol strapped to one hip, a large knife on the other, and carried a strange-looking rifle. When Troy looked at his weapon curiously, Charlie handed it over. "It's a cornershot," he explained."

"I've heard of these," Troy said with obvious awe as he took the rifle, "but I never got a chance to play with one."

"What's a cornershot?" Mary asked.

"It's designed to fold in the middle so you can shoot at a ninety-degree angle from where you're standing," Charlie explained. "Corner shot because you can shoot around corners."

"That's awesome," Jaime said. "That way,

you aren't in the line of fire when you're shooting it."

"Exactly." Charlie took the weapon back from Troy and showed them how he could flip a lever in the middle of the rifle, bend it to where he wanted it, and lock it in place.

"But how do you know what you're shooting at if you can't see your target?" Mary asked.

"Like this." He flipped a small screen out on the side of the rifle. "When you power it on, it'll show a video feed of whatever the barrel is pointed at." He flipped another switch to demonstrate. "See, it even has cross-hairs for targeting."

Troy took the rifle and stepped towards the hallway leading back to the elevator. He leaned his shoulder against the wall and maneuvered the weapon until he could see down the hall. "Hey, Joel, duck!"

A commotion sounded from the hallway and everyone rushed out to see what had happened. Joel climbed back to his feet from behind the equipment he had knocked over in his haste to take cover. "You're an ass, you know that?"

"Yeah, and you're late. That means you

don't get to play with the awesome gun," Troy pointed out as he stepped around the corner and switched the rifle until it was straight once more.

"Joel's here?" Todd barely glanced up from his preparations and didn't bother to wait for a response before continuing. "Good. I'm almost done. Are the rest of you all ready to go?"

"As ready as we're going to get, I guess," Marc said. "Troy, give him back his gun."

As Troy reluctantly handed the weapon back to Charlie, he pointed out, "Maybe you won't be as much of a hindrance as I thought." As Charlie strung the weapon across his shoulder by the attached strap, Troy sent another longing look at the gun. "Any possibility you have an extra one of those that I could borrow for a while?" he asked hopefully.

"No, this is the only one I have. But about my being a hindrance," he responded, "I know that you guys have been up against more of this type of thing than anyone else out there that I know of, so I'm prepared to follow your lead here. But at the same time, I just might surprise you in what I can help with."

"You're ready too?" Todd looked over at David. "You're still planning to roll out medical as soon as we leave, right?"

"Even if you all make it back fine, I'm going to want checkups on all of you, just in case."

"Sounds reasonable." Todd turned his attention back to his spell. With only a few muttered phrases that David didn't understand, he tossed a silvery powder at the mirror, which began to take on a silvery glow of its own. It brightened for only a moment, shining brilliantly enough to make the team cover their eyes before fading to a dull luster with barely a hint of the glow that had been so blinding only moments before. Vague shadows began to take shape behind the glass, murky at first but solidifying into dim, barely identifiable shapes.

With only a moment's hesitation, the team stepped towards the shimmering portal. Troy was the first to reach it and he put one hand out to touch the surface as he walked closer. As he reached the mirror's bounds, however, he stopped, his brow creasing in confusion. "It's solid."

"What?" Todd stepped up next to him and

reached out to touch the pane as well. He met resistance also and, as much as he pushed, the glass refused to give way. "I don't understand."

"What's happening?" David asked. "Is something wrong?"

Todd took a step back. "I messed up somewhere, just give me a minute..." he stepped over to his work table, mumbling to himself as he went.

Other members of the team pushed forward to touch the glass, which continued to shine but refused to give way. "I think I see something," Ty pointed out once he was close to the mirror. He pressed his face closer, straining to see what lay beyond the glass.

"What?" Everyone turned to look again, more closely this time. Those who had moved away from their vantage points scrambled to get as good of a view as they could. The shadowy shapes started to clarify and gather together, revealing a brightly-lit chamber beyond.

The chamber's walls and floor were stone, with hooks and rings attached all over the place. As they watched, a dark-haired man opened a door at the far end of the room and walked into view, dragging something on a long chain behind him.

Whatever he was dragging slid across the floor without much resistance as he pulled it over to a wall that held a couple of hooks. He looped the chain through a ring on the wall and pulled, hoisting his captive to her feet.

Everyone watching stepped closer as they recognized Jen, bloody, bruised, and very angry. They couldn't hear what the man was saying but she must not have liked what it was because while he spoke, she spat onto him. Though her eyes were swollen and bruised, there was no mistaking the fierce hatred that shone in them as the phlegm landed on the demon's face.

He reached out, hand like lightning, to slap her against the wall. Even though there was no sound, everyone winced from the impact.

Jen sagged on her chains as her head bounced off the wall and a growl sounded from the hybrids. Even Charlie, who had only seen Jen in photographs and video footage, seemed surprised at the spectacle.

The man secured Jen's hands and feet to the wall before heading out the same doorway he had brought her in through. When he returned moments later, he had another captive with him, this one crawling on hands and knees at the end of his chain. The demon suspended the new prisoner in the middle of the room, hanging him by his wrists from a horizontal bar at the end of yet another pair of chains so that he could swing freely.

From their vantage point on the far side of the mirror, none of the gathered spectators could identify the auburn-haired young man but by the expression of rage on Jen's face as she looked up, she recognized him. Even as the demon secured the young man into place, Jen began straining at her bonds and screaming, thrashing and wrenching at her chains. Her efforts were to no avail, as the demon ignored her outburst and concluded his task.

Once both prisoners were secured, the demon walked to a side wall and dragged an oddly-shaped wooden cart to the center of the room. He pulled a long, braided whip off the cart and stepped behind the hanging man. No sound was needed to hear the man's screams as the whip struck his flesh. Once, twice, three times the whip lashed across his back and the demon laughed silently beyond the glass. Jen, chained to the wall as she was, strained and thrashed at her bonds as she screamed at the demon.

Finally, with tears streaming down the chained man's face and his blood dripping into a glistening pool on the floor, the demon changed his attention to Jen. Leaving the bleeding man where he hung, he walked over to Jen and began to unhook her.

He hooked her hands together so that she couldn't use them and pulled her to the middle of the room, shoving her down to her knees in front of the hanging man. The demon pulled the chain that still led from the collar around her neck through a small ring in the floor and secured her in place.

Once she was locked into place, the demon went back to his rolling cart and pulled out another whip, this one with many lashes at the end of it. He spoke to Jen again, and by his scowl and narrowed eyebrows in addition to the flare of his nostrils, he wasn't pleased with the answer. Without missing a step, he swung the flogger, this time aiming for Jen.

Before the whip contacted, Todd, Patrick, Mary and Jaime turned away so that they wouldn't have to see. The growling that the hybrids had started at the beginning of the show intensified until David could almost believe that neither of them were hybrids at all but full-blooded werewolves in their own rights and were about to be released on a moon-fueled frenzy. Even the hairs on the back of Troy's shaggy mane appeared to be bristled as though his wolfish heritage was straining for release. Joel's eyes were as dark as a moonless night, his jaw clenched as tightly as his fists.

David looked in sympathy at Todd and the rest of Jen's family, understanding why they wouldn't want to see what was happening to their sister. To his surprise, Charlie also seemed to be more affected by the spectacle than David would have guessed, horror and anger warred across his face and his fists were tightly clenched at his sides in a surprising mimicry of the hybrid next to him. J.J. stood, watching in horror; both fists clenched so tightly around his rifle that David wouldn't have been surprised to see the metal begin to fail. His biceps bulged beneath his shirt and his eyes were narrowed to slits.

"Okay, that's enough." David's voice broke through the growling. "Can you turn this off?"

With a quick word and a couple of gestures, Todd banished the sight from the mirror, leaving only a thin haze of silvery light behind. His eyes shone brightly as tears flowed down his face but he didn't speak. His jaw was clenched tightly enough that the tendons on the side of his face showed prominently.

Still, nobody spoke and nobody moved. Even David was in shock at what he had seen. Although none of them had said as much, it had been generally understood that Jen was not in a good place and she was likely to be hurt pretty badly by the time they got her home. Despite that unspoken understanding, David had never even entertained the idea that something like what they had just witnessed would be happening to her.

Troy was the first to move. He stomped towards the stairs, ignoring the elevator altogether, and took them three and four at a time as he ascended to the ground floor. Joel wasn't far behind but for some reason, he didn't look as surprised as everyone else did.

David made a mental note to ask him why.

Just not right now.

Chapter 11

The beatings weren't that bad, Jen admitted to herself as she felt the flogger crack across her skin for the millionth or so time. What really bothered her was how much the asshole with the whip seemed to be enjoying what he was doing to her. As an additional bonus, however, Jen also knew that she was causing more trouble for him than usual.

She had been following the dreamwalker's instruction on how to draw the energy from her surroundings and the demons had quickly reacted. What she hadn't realized at first was that she was drawing the energy that they were trying to take into themselves. Although she doubted that they knew it was her siphoning the energy, she knew that they would figure it out soon enough. She just hoped that she would be able to figure out what to do with it once that happened.

The dreamwalker had given her more than information and instructions on how to draw in the energy. He had also given her hope. Someone out there knew where she was. Just that alone was enough to give her strength to face the demons for another few days, more than long enough to start stealing their power. Now, she just hoped that she could steal enough to slow them down, or at least make them lose some of the power that they held, not only over her but over the rest of the prisoners as well.

As she was dragged out into the torture room again, she felt the strangest sensation that she was being watched. Not wanting to let the demon know that she felt it, just in case he and the other demons were the cause, she looked around as she was hung against the wall, but she could see nothing that could be causing the feeling. Part of her hoped that it was the dreamwalker, checking back in with her or maybe even ready with information about what had happened to her team but a much larger part hoped that it wasn't him. She didn't want him, or anyone else, to see what was about to happen.

"I hope you're well rested," Cylin said as he attached her leash through a ring over her head and hoisted her to her feet. "Thaxter's looking forward to seeing you again."

Jen's lips curled into a sneer. "Thaxter should hook you up to a wall and beat you senseless. But then, you'd probably like it."

"Maybe," the demon admitted. "But not as much as your little friend does."

Jen knew that he could only be talking about one of the prisoners and hoped that she was wrong. Unable to come up with a suitably appropriate insult for the demon, she spat on him. Admittedly, the action was childish but she felt better as she saw the droplets of spittle pasted to the monster's face.

She wasn't left much time to gloat over her actions, however. Almost as soon as the phlegm made contact, Cylin lashed out and slapped her hard enough to slam her head against the wall behind her. "You will learn to behave," she heard his voice echo through the searing pain, "even if it takes the rest of your life, you will learn."

He left her there and went back into the dark room. Jen took the moment of peace to look around, waiting for the room to stop spinning from the impact of her head into the wall, because she still felt eyes boring into her skin. Careful to not move too quickly, she scanned the all-too-familiar room, searching for the cause but again came up empty-handed. "Is that you?" she asked, her lips barely moving as she muttered the almost-inaudible words.

She had half expected to see an illusion of her brother appear in the room. The sensation felt a lot like the feeling she got when Todd was watching her but this time was different somehow and she didn't really expect him to be the cause. She wasn't sure if she was relieved or disappointed when seconds passed and nothing happened. The room remained as bare as it had been when Cylin left and finally Jen had to admit that the sensation was likely just a figment of her imagination.

The demon came back into the room leading a young man on his leash. He was slightly shorter than Jen, with light auburn hair, sad brown eyes, and Jen swore under her breath as she recognized Bailey.

Of all the people that Cylin could have brought in, she hated it the most when he tortured Bailey in front of her. Bailey reacted much differently than the other men did, likely a reaction from being held prisoner for too long but she couldn't help feeling like she should do something about it. Every time he was brought back into the holding cell after a stint in the torture room, Baily would whimper at the sound of any movement nearby, traumatized as he was by his experiences with the demons.

Not that she didn't feel any different in that regard about the rest of the people held prisoner by the demons but there was something so fragile about Bailey that made her feel even more protective over him. Although she knew that it was futile, she shouted insults and slander at the demon, hoping to transfer at least some of his attention away from Bailey and onto her.

The wheels of the demon's implement cart rattled across the stone floor as he pulled it over to where Bailey hung in silence. Her howls increased as the whip cracked across his back. Cylin laughed, a sinister chuckle that reverberated throughout the room at her reaction, and whipped Bailey again.

She could almost feel when the demon began to draw the energy, it felt as though she was in a pool of swirling water and someone pulled the drain plug. As she felt it flow past her and towards the demon, Jen reached out with her mind as the dreamwalker had taught her and redirected it. She could feel immediately that the power flow changed but the demon was too involved in his entertainment to notice quite yet. As Bailey shrieked in agony, Jen struggled at her bonds, trying to wrench herself free and stop the demon before he did any more damage to the already broken man.

Even though she knew it was useless, she continued to fling slurs at the demon, insulting everything from his perverse sense of entertainment to his lineage, including the idea that he was nothing more than a high-school science experiment gone seriously wrong. Cylin just laughed at her and whipped Bailey hard enough to draw blood. As the crimson rivulets flowed down onto the floor, Jen could see the tears streaming down Bailey's face until finally the demon had enough. He turned towards Jen, who continued to shout meaningless insults.

Apparently, the demon had a good memory. The last time that he had left her hands unhooked, she had punched him in the face. Because of that, she had received one of the worst beatings yet but she still felt that it had been worth it. Now, however, he wasn't giving her the opportunity to repeat her actions. He unhooked her hands but kept hold of them in an iron grip until he had them hooked together so that she couldn't get a good swing on him. Once her hands were secure, he unhooked the leash where it was attached to the wall and dropped her unceremoniously onto the ground. As soon as her feet were unhooked as well, he dragged her towards Bailey without waiting to see if she would crawl. She hadn't crawled for either of the demons yet and she had given them no reason to believe that she would do so now.

He dragged her until she was at Bailey's feet and ran the chain from her collar through another ring, this time on the floor. He cinched her down until she could barely even kneel.

"Are you ready to submit?" Cylin asked her. As with the other times she had been asked, no explanation was given as to what they meant or what precisely they wanted from her.

"Screw you," she answered. She didn't bother to look up, she knew from all the other times she had been in that position that he was going to pull one of the torture implements from his cart and beat her with it. At least she had the relief of knowing that he would be hitting her instead of hurting Bailey any more right then. Not much of a success on her part but better than nothing. "I don't care what you want from me," she retorted. "As far as I'm concerned, you can kiss my ass."

Cylin didn't respond verbally; his answer was a snap of a whip across her back. Jen bit back a cry of pain with that strike but knew it was only a matter of time before the pain became too much. Instead, she focused on the energy that continued to swirl around her, drawing more of it into herself. She focused on the energy and drawing it in, keeping her attention on what she was doing instead of what the demon was doing to her.

To her surprise, the more energy she hijacked, the better she felt. She knew that she was still being whipped but all she could feel was pressure, not any pain. She had no idea how long Cylin continued to beat on her but finally he walked back over to the cart. She knew that it wasn't over; the demons weren't ever satisfied by just a short beating.

Before he returned to the beating, however, she could hear him greet someone out of her line of sight. "Just in time, I see." He spoke in the guttural-sounding language of the demons, and Jen knew without waiting to hear the newcomer's voice that Thaxter had arrived.

"Yes, it would appear so. How long have these two been here?"

"About a half hour or so, I'd guess," Cylin responded.

The pair stepped into Jen's view as they spoke. What little pain she felt was rapidly fading but she kept her head lowered as she listened to the demons' conversation.

Thaxter, a taller, strawberry-blonde version

of Cylin, sniffed at the air and swirled his hand around in a strange gesture. "I see the energy is still diminished," he observed.

Cylin nodded. "I'm pretty sure that this one is responsible."

"Absurd," Thaxter disagreed. "He's been here for far too long. If he had been capable of something like this, we would have known long ago."

"True. But the woman hasn't been here for very long at all."

"I see," the taller demon nodded. "And you are certain of this?"

"As sure as I can be. The energy anomaly only seems to occur near her. In fact, I believe she has only now stopped siphoning it."

The more often she heard the demonic language, the more Jen recognized. Now, she understood almost every word they said to each other, although she wasn't about to let them know and the words she didn't recognize, she could guess without much effort. Beyond that, Jen realized two things. First of all, they knew what she was up to and that it was her doing it. Secondly, somewhere in the middle of eavesdropping on their conversation, she had stopped taking in the energy. She debated on drawing more in, realizing that it would likely cause more trouble for her if she did but then decided that she didn't care. The demons hadn't killed her yet, although she had given them plenty of reason and she was fairly sure that they wouldn't kill her now. Silently she reached out to absorb more of the energy that swirled around the room.

"Any word on Vanitha?" That wasn't the first time Jen had heard that name and she had only recently confirmed that it belonged to the demoness who had captured her.

"Vanitha is no longer my concern. She was weak enough to allow a group of humans to capture her. As for this pet of hers, he'll just become a fountain of energy for us. Before too long we won't even have to do anything to re-trieve it."

Jen felt her blood boil as they spoke. She knew that they were discussing the damage that they had already done to Bailey and were planning to do further damage to him. Although she knew it was in vain, she lunged towards Cylin.

With both hands outstretched, she threw

herself at the demon, swinging at him as she went. She had forgotten about the chain that held her throat to the floor, however, and found herself being stopped far shorter than she had intended.

Cylin's eyes were widened in surprise as he looked down at her, his initial shock quickly flared into anger. His eyes on fire and his upper lip curled into a snarl, he reached without looking and pulled the first weapon he touched from the cart. The braided whip flew through the air and snapped against Jen's cheek. She howled as the pain seared through her face.

The demon whipped her until she could barely breathe and she could hear Bailey struggling against his chains as she lay curled up in a ball on the floor. Hot welts rose all over her skin and it felt as though there wasn't an inch of her that the whip couldn't reach.

"That's enough," Thaxter spoke up. He stepped forward and squatted down in front of Jen, who looked up at him in disdain. "You have been very naughty, haven't you?"

She spat at that demon as well and discovered that there was blood mixed in with the spittle this time. Cylin moved to lash her again but Thaxter held up a hand to stop him. "Has she been questioned about accepting my ownership of her?" Vaguely, Jen realized that the demons were speaking in their own, strange language to each other. She hadn't noticed immediately, as their language sounded as natural and comprehensible to her as her own native tongue.

"Every time. She has refused you each time she is asked."

Thaxter swore. "Has she been willing to do anything that could be considered acceptance?" When Cylin shook his head, he swore again, some of the wrath fading from his eyes. "You said she heals quickly?"

He didn't answer but just pointed down at her. Thaxter looked down as well and his eyebrows shot up again. "Already?"

"They seem to be healing faster every time she is wounded."

"And have you been harming her further, to see how far this healing ability of hers will work?"

"Yes. So far, the longest time she has taken

to recover is overnight." Cylin looked back up at the larger incubus. "Do you think that is why they wanted her?"

"I have no idea. Has she shown any other special ability?"

He shook his head. "She continues to talk to the others but that is not uncommon."

"Does she heal the others as she does herself?"

"No. She shows obvious signs of unhappiness when we put someone back into the room with her after a beating but she has done nothing to heal any but herself."

Thaxter's cold stare traveled over Jen's limp form for a long moment, pausing to admire the collection of bruises and watching them slowly heal. "Perhaps she is a psychic after all."

Cylin shook his head. "No. I had her appraised as soon as she was brought in, as you asked. She has no abnormal abilities that our appraiser was able to detect."

Thaxter raised his eyebrows at the smaller demon. For a moment, Jen was surprised at how much these vile creatures could seem like humans. "Fine, then. You have another week to make her submit." He turned to walk out of the room. "Be aware," he called over his shoulder as he left. "If you fail at this, I will have no choice but to turn her over to the Inquisitors and then we'll have to explain to them why we weren't able to do our jobs."

Cylin visibly paled at the mention of Inquisitors, his dark hair standing out in even starker contrast against his fear-lightened skin and Jen made a mental note to try and find out who, or what, the Inquisitors were. The term seemed familiar to her but she wasn't sure where she had heard it and she couldn't exactly ask the demons for more details. The last thing she wanted was to let them know she was on to them. As she watched the sunset-haired demon walk out of the torture room, Jen realized that she no longer had the feeling of being watched. Maybe, she thought to herself, it had been Thaxter watching her.

His voice floated back into the room after he was gone. "Or, rather, why YOU failed. Do not fail me in this, my protégé. I will not be denied this at your hands."

As soon as Thaxter was gone, Cylin got busy.

He unhooked Bailey first and led him, shaky and unsteady even on his knees, to the holding cell. Small smears of blood testified to the path the pair took, shining in the dim light. While they were gone, Jen examined her legs, hips and arms. She wondered if there were any marks left but all she was able to discover were a handful of faint pink and white areas where the skin hadn't completely healed.

When Cylin came back into the room, Jen expected to be taken back into the dark room as well but that was not to be the case. He walked past her without even looking at her direction and went out the same door that Thaxter had left through. Jen watched him, curious. She was rarely left alone, so she didn't really believe that he was going to just leave her there, so she wondered what the despicable demon was up to.

When he came back in, he was pulling what appeared to be a sawhorse behind him. He brought this latest piece of equipment over next to where Jen still lay on the ground and locked the wheels into place. "Are you ready to submit to your new master?" He asked without looking at her.

"Not a chance," Jen retorted.

"I was hoping you'd say that," he answered.

Chapter 12

While Todd flipped through the pages of his spell book, David stood back with the rest of the group to give him some room to work. He wasn't sure what had gone wrong with the first attempt at the planar travel spell but he could almost feel the anticipation building in the team as they waited for their chance to exact some revenge. It was like a not-quite-audible buzz, a humming in the air that vibrated from person to person, causing them to grow antsier by the moment. None of them even considered the possibility that Todd would be unable to open a gate to Jen. It was simply unacceptable.

He knew that other people on the team had seen the demon before; after all they had been there when Jen was taken. The brief view that he had witnessed through the glass at Todd's first attempt was the first time that David had seen the demon and he was surprised at how normal the creature looked. Even though he knew that some demons could pass as human, just as the succubus in the sub-basement could, it still shook him to know that he could easily walk past the demon on the street and not know it.

He considered that possibility for a long moment. How many times had he seen a demon? he wondered. Were any of the people that he thought he knew even people? Sure, he was the most comfortable with humans and neither werewolves nor vampires caused any fear to rise in him but he shuddered at the idea that there might actually be demons out in the town at that moment, with none of them the wiser. How could he and his team, he silently wondered, even hope to identify one when they found one? Was there a trick to it?

When his phone rang, it was a welcome distraction from the almost palpable tension in the room and the disturbing turn that his thoughts had taken. He glanced at the phone but before answering he turned to Marc. "Let me know if anything happens."

When Marc nodded, David stepped a few feet away from the group and answered his phone. He had told Kelly to hold all of his calls until he told her different so whatever had driven her to interrupt must be important.

"There's someone here to see you," She explained. "I think you need to speak with him."

"We're still kind of busy down here," David replied, trying to keep the irritation from his voice. The last thing he wanted was to be pulled away at this critical junction. "Can it wait?"

"He says no," she answered. "And I'm guessing that things haven't quite gone according to plan, because there haven't been any medical teams showing up yet."

David sighed. "No, something didn't work right, so the plan's on hold for the moment." He looked over to where Todd was frowning and writing in a small notebook. "But it looks like I might have a couple minutes before we try it again."

"In that case, you might want to meet with this man. He says it's about Jen."

David glanced around the group. With the image of Jen removed from the mirror, they had started to calm down, so he didn't want to say anything that could rile them up again. "Fine. I'll be up in a few minutes. Where is he?"

"I'll send him up to your office."

As David hung up the phone, he started towards the elevator. Halfway there, he was joined by Charlie, who was still dressed in his battle gear. "What's going on?"

David shrugged. "Since it appears that Todd needs a little more time to get everything ready, I have some work I need to get caught up on." He could tell that Charlie knew he wasn't being honest but appreciated the NPIB agent for not calling him on it in front of his men. As the elevator doors closed behind them, David turned towards Charlie's questioning gaze.

"There's someone here claiming to have information about Jen," he explained. "I didn't want to say anything in front of the team; they're already worked up enough as it is."

"Sounds reasonable. Who is it?"

"I have no idea; Kelly didn't say." When the doors opened, they were on the third floor and

David led the way down the hall to his office. Inside, a small man with dark hair and round, wire-framed glasses was sitting in a chair in front of David's desk, quietly sipping at a cup of coffee. He stood up and turned towards the men as they entered, his freshly-shaven smile fading as he discovered that David wasn't alone.

"I hadn't realized you were busy," he said as he set his cup down on the desk. "I can wait until you are finished with your business."

"No, it's all right," David answered. "This is Charlie Winters, he's with the NPIB. How can I help you?"

The visitor shook his head and stepped closer to the door. "I had meant to speak with you privately, so I will just wait outside."

"Then you're going to be waiting a while," David pointed out. "Charlie's been here for a while now and I doubt he plans to leave any time soon." He stepped closer to the smaller man. "Besides, if this is about Jen, I'd rather hear about it as soon as possible."

"I can understand that, but I'm not sure I trust the wisdom of discussing this in front of larger ears," the man explained, looking pointedly at Charlie as he spoke.

"I understand," Charlie said as he comprehended the man's concerns. "But whatever you say can be kept confidential. Right now, we're just worried about getting Jen back."

The man looked at him appraisingly before sending a questioning look over to David. "You, she trusts, so I know I can trust you as well. This one she's never mentioned, so I'm not so sure I can trust him to be silent over all of this."

"She's never met him," David explained. "Charlie arrived after Jen was taken and he's been trying to help us get her back."

The man eyed Charlie suspiciously. "And what is your interest in her?" Before Charlie could speak, he raised a hand. "And don't bother with whatever lie you were about to tell me; I can see when you are truthful."

"If you can see when I'm being honest then you know I'm telling you the truth when I say that I will keep whatever you are here to say confidential."

The visitor scanned Charlie's face for a long moment, searching his eyes and the rest of his features for any signs of deception. Finally he nodded and walked back over to pick up his coffee. After taking another drink, he looked over at David. "I suppose I should begin by introducing myself, as we haven't met in person. My name is Steve Jenkins."

"I thought your voice was familiar. How was your rest?"

"It was enjoyable, thank you, although I do wish I had been here to help when Jen was taken." He sat in the same chair that he had been previously occupying and took another drink of his coffee. "I hadn't realized that anything had happened to her until she contacted me the other day." Smiling ruefully into his mug, he added, "While the rest was nice, I can't help but feel guilty about lying in bed asleep while all of this was going on outside my knowledge."

Charlie closed the door and took a seat in the other chair in front of David's desk. Once everyone was seated, he motioned for Steve to continue. "I had intended on following the situation more closely and I apologize for my late involvement. However, I wanted to tell you in person that Jen is alive, albeit quite angry, and that I have spoken with her."

"I appreciate your telling us about this in person. The doctors at the hospital wouldn't let me talk to you for very long, no big surprise considering your condition."

Steve waved off his concern. "My condition wasn't as bad as they assumed. For some reason, they believed that I was on the brink of death but I was in nowhere near that much peril. Jen, on the other hand, is in very dire straits indeed."

"We are aware of that as well," David explained. "Her brother was able to pull up an image of her situation this morning." He folded his hands on his desk. "We are doing everything we can to bring her home."

"I believe you are," Steve replied, his eyes traveling from one man to the next, "and I wish that there was more I could do to help in that. But I'm afraid that my abilities do not allow me to transport people from one place to another, all I can do is look in on her when she needs me.

"However, I was also able to describe to her

how to absorb the energy around her and draw it into herself." Before either of the men could object, he raised a hand. "I realize how dangerous that is, on many levels. She is untrained in how to use the energy that she is absorbing and she is in Derathim where the only energy available to her is dark energy. However, I believe that there was no other choice but to teach her to draw on the energy there. If she is to survive, she will need to use every opportunity that presents itself to her."

"Wait a minute," David interrupted. "How could she draw energy? Don't you have to be a psychic or a mage to do that?"

"Exactly. I'm not sure why she wasn't trained but she seemed to be unaware of her own ability." He took another drink of his coffee. "But there is a bigger problem with all this."

"What's that?" Charlie asked.

"She'll likely come out tainted by the darkness. There's no avoiding it, her exposure has already been far too long and the more time she spends there, the worse her exposure will be."

"And I'm sure that the energy she's absorbing while she's there isn't helping very much either," David muttered. "So how bad should we expect this to be?"

"There's no real way to tell," Stave shrugged. "For most people, even minimal exposure to dark energy is enough to damage them for life. To actively absorb it as I have instructed Jen to do would normally be half a step away from outright suicide. However, there have been occasions where people have been in extended contact with beings from the dark plane without long-term effects, so that gives me hope. Jen's strong. While I wouldn't expect her to overcome the taint on her own, given enough time and proper treatment, I think that she should be able to overcome its effects."

"I guess that's some good news," David said as he poured a cup of coffee for himself and topped off Steve's as well. He didn't like that this added a whole new element of risk to an already dangerous situation but he had to believe that it could be fixed later. One problem at a time, that was how he intended to proceed. "On a different note, I know she isn't in a very good situation but how does she seem to be holding up mentally?" he asked. "I'm not sure how long you were able to talk with her but I figured I had to ask."

"She seems to be all right, for the moment," he replied. "She was pretty upset and angry but that's to be expected." Steve thought for a moment before adding, "I have to admit, she also seemed to be scared, although she was trying to hide it." He chuckled. "When you invite a dreamwalker into your head, it's amazing how little you can keep hidden."

He sighed and took a drink of his freshened cup. "That was one of the reasons I taught her to draw the energy," he finally admitted. "If she has something to focus on, she is less likely to succumb to despair while in the demon's grasp." He looked up at David. "I had also hoped that if she was to manage to pull some of the demon's energy from him, his hold over her would lessen, thus making her retrieval easier." He lowered his eyes again. "I wasn't sure how close anyone was on a retrieval plan so I didn't explain that part to her. I didn't want to get her hopes up too far until I knew whether you would be able to get her back."

"We are doing everything we can," Charlie explained.

"I'm sure you are," Steve said, looking over at him as he answered. "But you need to understand that she's not going to be in any condition to go through your decontamination processes when she returns. If you try to force her into one, it'll likely kill her."

"Todd is still working on his spell; he is trying to open a gate so that the team can go through to get her," David explained. "We had hoped to have her back by now but the spell didn't work the way he had planned."

"If there is anything I can do to assist in this, please let me know," Steve requested. "After all, I owe her my life. The least I can do is assist in saving hers."

At Charlie's look of confusion, David explained. "You read through Jen's files, haven't you?" When Charlie nodded, he explained. "Steve was the dreamwalker that was possessed by a demon not too long ago, the one that drew your agency's attention to Jen in the first place."

He looked up in surprise. "I almost forgot."

He rifled through the stacks of paperwork that had accumulated on his desk. "Sahara talked to someone that might have a way to get past the demons' mental powers. Where is that report?" He pushed a stack off to the side and pulled more papers towards him. Pulling a sheet from close to the bottom of the stack, he smiled. "Here we are!"

"Sahara Peters, one of Jen's close friends, has been doing some research on her own. She met another paranormal investigator of some variety, one that doesn't seem to be affiliated with any agency on record, who had some interesting information.

"Apparently this investigator had also come into contact with the succubus we captured. He described her perfectly and attributed his resistance to her charms to an amulet that he wears. This amulet of his supposedly has the blood of another demon inside it and the more powerful demonic blood is supposed to cancel out the lesser magic of the lesser demon." He looked up from the paper and met Charlie's eyes. "I wonder how well this type of protective charm would work."

Steve shrugged. "As far as I'm aware, nobody has caught a demon in quite a few years. Without a live demon, there isn't any way to run tests on something like that." Even the demon that had been inhabiting Steve's body when he had first met Jen had been killed. Steve himself had begged for death, offering himself as a sacrifice so that the demon could be eliminated.

Jen, however, had refused to kill him. She and her team had come up with an amazingly clever way of removing the demon from Steve's body, leaving him relatively intact in the process. Looking back at the difficulty in killing that demon, he could understand whole-heartedly why capturing a demon was out of the question. He of all people knew how dangerous they could be.

David shook his head. "The demoness that initially captivated my team is locked up downstairs."

Now it was Charlie's turn to look shocked. "I had thought that she'd been taken away already. My team should have been here to retrieve her a week ago."

"Nobody's gotten here to claim her," David

responded. "I'd hoped that she would be able to help us figure out where Jen was. Unfortunately, nobody has been able to get close enough to find anything out from her."

"Why not?"

"Because all of the people left on my team are men and they are susceptible to her magic. I have a female officer on loan from another department right now and she keeps everyone out of the demoness's cell."

"Since you have one available, it seems like a good enough way to test the theory," Steve offered. "Use some of her blood and send one of the men in on a tether."

David considered the idea for a moment before agreeing. "That sounds like a reasonable idea. Now I just need to figure out a way to get the blood out of her in the first place."

"Maybe we should talk to the team," Steve suggested. "One of them may have a sugges-tion."

David agreed, so he, Charlie, and the dreamwalker headed downstairs. There, they found the team milling about as Todd sat against a wall and muttered to himself, his eyes slightly glazed in a combination of exhaustion and extreme focus. Not wanting to disturb the mage, David signaled for the team to join him in the meeting room.

Once everyone was gathered, David explained. "While Todd is busy working on his spell, we have come up with a possible way to reduce or avoid the effects of the demons' magic. We need to get some blood from the demoness we have in custody but in order to do that we need to send someone in after it." He looked around at the gathered men in the room. "As I'm sure you realize, we can't send any of you into the cell with her because of the mental abilities the demon possesses. Nor am I willing to send either of Jen's sisters in with her, although I am reasonably sure that they wouldn't suffer the effects of the succubus's thrall.

"The only other females available to us are Kelly, who has refused to go anywhere near the demon, and Theo, who is on loan and can't be expected to go into a possibly dangerous situation for us."

"We could just stand in the doorway and

shoot her," J.J. suggested. "She'll still bleed if she's shot, won't she?"

Troy shook his head. "No, shooting her won't hurt enough. I've got a baseball bat."

"I like the baseball bat," Ty added. "But personally, I like the idea of a good, old-fashioned shank."

"Come on, guys, you know that none of you will be allowed down to where she's being held," Marc interrupted as more people started to shout ideas, each one more outrageous than the last. He held up a hand as the group protested his interruption. "I have a suggestion you'll probably all appreciate, if you'll hear me out."

David stepped closer to Marc to encourage him. "What's your idea?"

"I think we should have Theo do it." Before David could protest, he continued. "We give her a net launcher, that'll restrain the demon and minimize the threat. To take that a step further, once she's restrained, she can use one of the werewolf tranquilizers to sedate her even more. Either that'll knock her out or it'll calm her down but either way it'll be easier for Theo to step inside with a syringe to get the blood."

David started to nod as Marc described his plan. "That sounds like it could work," he commented once Marc finished. "But I'll still need to clear that by Theo and make sure she's agreeable to it." Since Theo wasn't a regular member of the New World team, or even an employee of the company, her compliance was nowhere near guaranteed. David didn't want to agree to anything involving her until he had her consent.

He started towards the elevator, but stopped halfway down the hall and returned to the meeting room. He snagged Marc by an arm and pulled him out of the room as well. "If she doesn't like your idea, I'd rather she beat you for it, not me."

When they arrived at the basement, David called ahead for Theo to come out and meet with them. She slowed as she approached, looking nervously between the two men. "Have I done something wrong?" she asked as she stopped in front of them.

"No, nothing like that," David reassured her.

"We're actually here to see if you would be willing to help us out with something."

When she agreed to hear the plan, Marc explained about his idea. She nodded thoughtfully as he spoke but when he was finished, she looked uncertain. "I haven't ever used your team's equipment before, so I'd need to have someone explain how to use a net launcher but I'd guess your tranquilizer guns are pretty much the same as everyone else uses, right?" Her time with the police department had given her plenty of opportunities to use tranquilizers, so she felt reasonably confident on that portion of the plan. The net launchers were her only real concern, as they were specialized equipment that was mainly used by response teams. The police didn't have any, as far as she knew, and she had only seen them used once.

"The launcher's actually pretty easy to use, so if you're willing to try it, I can give you a rundown on how it works this afternoon."

Theo agreed and looked up at David. "Is this plan supposed to help get your person back somehow?" When he nodded as well, she smiled at them. "Sounds like a plan. When did you want to do this?" Though she didn't want to appear overly eager, she was already excited about the idea. The time she had spent working with the New World team had given her a new appreciation for, and a lot more insight into, the inner workings of how a response company actually worked. Had it not been for her volunteering to work this assignment, she never would have guessed how much was really involved. Secretly, she believed that working for a response team was a lot more exciting than filing useless reports down at her station, which was what most of her workday normally consisted of.

"As soon as possible," David answered. He peered down the hall towards the succubus's cell. The demoness could not be seen from his vantage point, which David had done intentionally. He didn't want any of his men to be accidentally overtaken by the creature. "Is she alright for the moment?"

"Yeah. I just checked on her a few minutes before you guys came down here so she should be fine for a while yet." She checked the clock on the wall before adding, "My next check-in on her isn't for another forty minutes."

"Okay then, why don't you come with us?" Marc and David led her up a floor to the team's training area. Instead of turning towards the meeting area and space where Todd was continuing to research his spell, they turned towards the firearm training area. Inside, Marc opened one of the weapon lockers and pulled out a net launcher, a tranquilizer gun, and ammunition for both. After securing the locker again, he explained to Theo how to use the launcher and showed her how to load and unload both weapons. As she had suspected earlier, the tranquilizer gun and darts were standard issue, and therefore were weapons she had used before. There were no surprises. The net launcher, on the other hand, was much lighter than she had expected, despite its bulk. The suppression weapon was in no way small, being over two and a half feet long and the barrel was almost a full three inches in diameter.

"Once it's loaded," he explained to her, "all you have to do is point it at the target. The canister will pop open to release the net once you fire it and then all you have to do is wait for the bolas to tie up the demon." The cartridge was large as well, looking in Theo's estimation almost too large to fit into the breach. It fit in easily, she was pleased to discover as she followed Marc's instruction to load and unload it.

"Sounds pretty simple," Theo agreed. "And you said there wasn't anything special about the tranquilizer, right?"

"That's right. This is a pretty standard issue weapon. It's not upgraded like the ones we use now but we always keep a few of these on standby in case of emergency."

"That makes sense." She examined the rifle and launcher for a few moments before pronouncing them good enough. "Besides," she added as she slung the launcher over her shoulder by its strap, "If I ever want to move up to a team like this one, being able to say that I've fired these at least once will look pretty good on me." She chuckled and headed for the door.

"Wait," Marc called after her. "You're going to need a syringe to get the blood from her."

"Right," She stopped and turned back towards him. "I almost forgot the most important part."

Marc smiled at the obviously excited woman as he screwed a needle onto the tip of an empty syringe. "You were thinking about applying to a response team?"

She shrugged noncommittally. "I'd thought about it. I know that the stuff I've been doing hasn't exactly been standard response procedure but it's been a hell of a lot better than riding a desk like I normally do."

"It can be pretty dangerous, though. I'm sure by now you have an idea of what's going on."

"Yeah, I've been catching bits and pieces about what happened to your missing teammate." She accepted the syringe that he held out to her. "That was actually what got me thinking about applying. It seems like you guys are a lot more open-minded about letting women onto your team, which is a lot better than most places around here."

Marc chuckled as he led her back towards the elevator. "Yeah. I think most of the other teams out there just haven't realized exactly how dangerous some women can be. Piss one of us off and we'll go bitch about it over a beer and be done with it by the next day. Piss one of you off, though, you plot revenge."

Theo snickered as she stepped onto the elevator behind him. "I was just thinking that if you had another woman on the team and something came up where Jen wasn't available again, you wouldn't have to go out and borrow someone you didn't know. I mean, even if you had someone on call, it seems like that would work out better for you."

"You do have a good point. Have you men-tioned this to David?"

She shook her head. "No, I didn't want to seem like I was trying to push my way in while everything was all screwed up."

When the door opened on Theo's floor, she stepped out of the elevator, leaving Marc where he was. "I'll let you know when I'm done."

"I'll be right here," he answered. "If you have any trouble at all, just back away. I don't want you to get hurt over this; it's not worth it."

"Don't worry," she reassured him. "I'll be fine." She headed down the hall towards the succubus's cell. Despite her assurance to the contrary, Theo was a bit nervous about the task she had agreed to. Though she had been watching over the demoness since her arrival at the New World office building, as she did every day, and there had been no problems, there was something decidedly creepy about the succubus. She was hiding something, Theo could tell, and a portion of her was frightened to discover what that secret might be – and if it would hurt her.

Marc stepped off the elevator and walked into the guard room which had live video footage of the demoness's cell. David was already inside, monitoring the prisoner. "Hey, boss," Marc greeted him. "She should be in there any second now."

As he spoke, the door to the cell opened on the small screen and Theo stepped inside. She was no longer holding the tranquilizer rifle at the ready that she had been carrying only moments before but instead held the net launcher, set and ready to use.

As the succubus stood up to rush at her, another futile effort to escape, Theo fired.

Since the succubus was moving towards the

doorway where Theo stood, she was only a few feet away when the woman fired the weapon. The canister shot out but the demon was too close for the net to be released from the canister. Instead, the steel cartridge slammed into the demon's face, knocking her backwards with the impact.

Theo looked over at the demon in surprise and then down at the launcher in her hands. Although Marc had explained that the net released a few inches past the barrel once the cartridge was triggered, she hadn't expected for the shot to have been so traumatic. She sent a quick glance at the camera, towards the men she knew to be watching, and shrugged. Slipping a hand into her pocket, she withdrew the syringe and walked over to the unconscious succubus.

"She's pretty good," Marc pointed out to David as they watched. "I wonder how long she still has left on her contract with the police department."

"I'm not sure how much longer she's got but you're right." He looked over at his unit leader. "You think she'd be interested?"

Marc nodded without taking his eyes off the monitor. "She mentioned something about it earlier. She didn't want to pressure you, considering everything else you've got going on right now. But I think that she'd be willing to consider an offer."

David looked back at the screen, watching Theo as she filled the syringe with the demon's blood. "She's got the attitude for it, I'll give her that." As Theo headed for the door, David looked over at Marc again. "I'll look into it; see if I can run her past the board."

"Take this video with you," Marc suggested, "and the one of her cuffing Troy to the light fixture. If nothing else, that'll give them a good laugh."

The men snickered as Theo walked into the guard room and held out the filled syringe. "Is there anything else you need?"

"Nope," David answered as he took the vial of blood. "Thank you for your help on this."

"Any time," she answered as she handed the weapons over to Marc. "If you need anything else, let me know."

Chapter 13

The spell wasn't finished by late that evening when Todd had to call it quits for the night. Even if he spent the rest of the night working on the problem at hand, it wouldn't do any good if he was too exhausted to hold the spell together. As much as he didn't want to leave Jen in the horrible situation she was in, he had no other choice.

By the time he got back to Jen's house, there was a plate of food wrapped and waiting for him with his name on a sticky note in the refrigerator. He recognized the handwriting on it as Mary's and he made a mental note to thank her for the meal later. At the sight of the food, even without any idea what it was, his stomach reminded him quite loudly how long it had been since his last meal. As usual, his magical work had engrossed him thoroughly enough that he had forgotten completely about dinner, let alone lunch. The only reason he had eaten breakfast that morning was because Mary had shoved a bowl of eggs, tomatoes, and bacon into his hands.

He heated the plate in the microwave and wandered through the house as he ate, wondering how he was going to be able to fix the spell. He had an idea of where he had gone wrong, he had felt it even while he was still in the process of casting but he wasn't sure how to fix it. Even worse, he wasn't sure that he had enough magical power to control the spell, even if he did manage to cast it correctly.

That was the part that perturbed him the most. He knew that everyone, Jen particularly, was relying on him to be able to open the portal so that they could commence their rescue. The idea that he wasn't powerful enough, that his twin sister – the other half of his soul – was currently and would continue to be suffering because of his inadequacy pissed him off. Not for the first time, and he doubted that it would be the last time, he resisted the urge to smash something. Standing in place for a long moment, breathing deeply to calm himself, he reminded himself that everything around him that he could break belonged to his sister and if he broke any of it, she would be seriously upset with him.

He choked back an involuntary sob. He would give anything, anything at all, just to have Jen back. Mad at him or not, he just wanted her home.

He rinsed off his plate and put it and his fork into the dishwasher, added some soap and got the machine running. As he headed towards the bedroom to get some sleep, there was a knock on the front door. Swearing softly, he turned to answer it.

On the front porch was a pair of men dressed in charcoal-colored suits. Both of the men had the same type and color of suit, tie, and shoes, and they were even about the same height and size. The biggest difference between them was that one was light haired and the other had brown hair. "Do you mind if we come in?" The blond asked as he opened a badge that identified him as belonging to the NPIB.

"Can it wait until morning?" Todd asked. "I've had a bit of a long day."

"I'm sure you have," the other one answered. "But we need to speak with you about Ms. Rice."

"She's not home."

Both of them chuckled, although Todd wasn't sure what was so funny. As far as he was concerned, there wasn't a single amusing thing in the situation they were in and the unexpected presence of the NPIB was even less so. "We are aware she's not here. That's why we want to talk with you about her."

"There isn't a lot I can tell you," Todd explained, refusing to step aside and let them in. He knew that it would likely be a bigger problem later that he hadn't willingly let them inside, but he hoped that he would be able to get Jen back before it became that much of an issue. Although the NPIB liked to throw their not-inconsiderable weight around, Todd knew that he wasn't required to cooperate with them until they either showed him a court order forcing his hand or he received a message from his company demanding that he cooperate. Considering he was technically on vacation, even an order from his boss didn't mean his compliance was mandatory.

With the mood he was still in, cooperation wasn't very high on his agenda.

Even then, he was pretty certain that he wouldn't have to allow them inside unless they had a court document that specifically allowed them to enter. This wasn't his house; he wasn't on the lease and he wasn't technically a resident. At most, he was a visitor. "You can come back and talk to her when she's here."

"I'm afraid you don't understand. We are here because we were informed that she was kidnapped and we want to try and find a way to locate her."

The brunette tried to step around Todd to enter the house but he refused to budge. "Do you have an entry order?"

"Son, are you aware of who we are?" the blond asked. "We're with the National Paranormal Investigative Board. Do you really want to do this?"

Todd grinned at them. He had never been a fan of the NPIB and having this opportunity to poke at them gave him a small amount of satisfaction. "Yeah, I think I do."

The dark-haired agent pulled a small notebook and a pen from a pocket inside his jacket. "Perhaps I should get your name so I can have it specifically added to the court order you seem to want so much." He flipped the notebook open and looked over at Todd expectantly.

Todd's eyes darkened as he gathered a small amount of his magical energy. He summoned one of his personal business cards from his desk and held it out for the officer. "My name is Todd Rice, Senior Magical Development and Research Specialist for Viceroy." Todd rarely threw around his name and rank, as it tended to intimidate people but at that moment it seemed like the best thing to do. The NPIB agents were obviously not above using intimidation tactics to get their way, so he figured that what was fair practice for them was fair practice for him. "Perhaps I should ask you if *you* are really sure you want to do this."

The agent looked down at the card in his

hand. Many of Viceroy's mages covered their business cards in a minor illusion, partially to reinforce the fact that it was indeed a mage's business card and partly to reduce the possibility of counterfeiting. Todd's was no different, shimmering slightly as though it had been coated in an oil slick. "You work for Viceroy?" He glanced up at Todd in surprise. Seemingly unawares of what he was doing, he rubbed his fingers over the card. It was a movement that Todd had seen plenty of times before because the visual appearance of the cards led many people to assume that there was a similar tactile sensation involved. It was one of the reasons that was his favorite design.

"You can call and verify that if you want to but I wouldn't recommend it." He checked his watch. "At least, not right now. It's about midnight where the director is and he doesn't appreciate being woken up over trivial complaints." Senior specialists reported only to the research director of Viceroy, a man who was almost legendary for his grumpiness at being woken over minor matters.

The more Todd thought about it, the more

he hoped that one of them would actually make the call.

As the agents looked at each other, as if they were trying to decide what to do, a car pulled up and parked at the curb behind their cruiser. Troy shut off the engine and climbed out, holding a bag from Taco King. "Sorry, I couldn't handle any more of that stuff Mary made. It was just too healthy," he snickered as he walked up towards the house. "Who're these guys?"

"Leaving," Todd answered with no inflection in his voice but a raised eyebrow at the unwanted visitors. "Right?"

The men backed off the porch, making sure to give Troy enough room to get past them. "We'll be in touch," the light-haired agent called back to Todd as they headed for their car.

"You do that," he called back. "But I would recommend getting in touch with a judge first; that's the only way you'll ever see the inside of this house." As soon as Troy was inside, Todd slammed the door and locked the deadbolt, intentionally making as much noise about it as possible.

"What was that all about?" Troy asked as he

put the bag on the coffee table. He looked at Todd in confusion. "Were they here about Jen?"

Todd nodded and peeked into the bag. "They were NPIB, here to snoop around where they don't need to be." He pulled out a burrito and sniffed at it. As he pulled off the wrapper, he looked up at Troy. "Damn, I hate those guys. Having one of them here snooping is bad enough but it was only a matter of time before he brought in more of his cronies."

Troy eyed him curiously as he pulled out another burrito. "Why do you hate them so much?"

"It's a long story," Todd explained as he took a bite of his burrito, "but a lot of the NPIB agents get away with a lot more than they should, just because most people don't know what they're really allowed to do." He took another bite and chewed thoughtfully. "And what they aren't. I think that's a bigger part."

"But you seem to be getting along with Charlie better than you did earlier."

"Yeah, I suppose that's because it's easier to deal with just one than it is to deal with a whole squad of them." He looked over at Troy.

"Be careful about what you tell them and what you let them get away with. They need to follow procedures just like everyone else. Just because people believe that the NPIB is above the law, that doesn't mean they really are." He finished his burrito in two more quick bites and threw the wrapper in the trash. "I should go to bed. If I'm going to pull that spell off tomorrow, I'll need to get some sleep."

"Hey, Todd," Troy called out as the mage headed for the bedroom. "Do you think they're going to try and stop you tomorrow?"

Todd shook his head without turning around. "If they stop me before I actually do anything, they won't be able to do anything to me. It's not illegal to think about doing something illegal, not even illegal to make a plan for it. Laws only come into play when action starts on a plan. If they let me cast it, then they can come after me." He stepped into his sister's bedroom and closed the door behind him.

The next morning, Todd called everyone back to the meeting area. "I think I figured out what went wrong," he explained to them. "I should be able to get it right this time."

"Before you do," David interrupted, "I have something for everyone." He held out a handful of small tags, each smeared with a red substance, on thin chains. "These should help you resist the demon's thrall. We don't know how well each of you will react to the demonic magic so I would rather take the extra step to keep you all safe." He handed the necklaces out to everyone who was planning on going through the mirror. After everyone had their chains around their necks, David had one necklace left, which he handed to Marc. "This one is for Jen. Get it to her as soon as you can; she's the most vulnerable."

Marc accepted the chain and dropped it around his neck as well. Once everyone had their protective amulets in place, they stepped forward to face the mirror again.

Todd had spent the last two hours clearing his mind of all the turmoil that had restricted him from being able to cast the spell earlier. The vision of his sister being beaten still haunted him, his dreams filled with the memory of what he had witnessed, but he drew strength from the image. He couldn't leave her there to suffer for another night, another hour, another minute.

He would get her out of that waking nightmare and he would do it now.

He felt the familiar warm tingling sensation as his magical glow brightened, filling him completely and stretching out from his fingertips and the top of his head. He uttered the incantation that he had spent the last couple of weeks studying, not needing to look at the book to remember how the spell was worded. Despite his certainty that the spell was well-memorized, he kept the book nearby. He didn't want to take any chances of needing it and not having it available.

As he spoke, he could feel the walls between the worlds weaken. Pressure closed in around him, as though he was gaining altitude too quickly. When he opened his eyes at the climax of the spell, the surface of the mirror had turned translucent silver.

It didn't look much different than it had the last time he had tried the spell but this time it felt less solid, less real, and he knew that the spell had worked. He breathed a silent sigh of relief and stepped closer to the mirror to pass through it.

Other members of the team stepped closer as well and he could feel them press closer as everyone was eagerly moving to retrieve Jen. When he placed a hand on the gate, however, Todd realized that there was a problem.

All of his magical skill, all of his power, had been poured into the spell.

It wasn't enough.

The portal gave way and he knew that it wasn't anywhere near as solid as it had been during the failed attempt. This time, however, instead of feeling like pushing through room-temperature water, it felt like he was trying to step through plastic wrap. It gave some as he pushed but there was too much resistance to make it through. "No," he whispered to himself. "It has to work; this can't happen."

"What's going on?" J.J. called up to him. "Why aren't we going through?"

"Looks like it didn't work again," Mike pointed out.

"NO!" Todd howled, his voice echoing through the room as he pounded on the paper-thin barrier between him and his twin sister. As hard as he pushed, both physically and magically, the wall wouldn't budge. He pounded on the wall until his hands were numb before leaning his forehead against the barrier, tears streaming down the glass.

He could see Jen on the other side, in the same room as she had been in the last time had seen her. She was chained down on her stomach, strapped to some sort of bench, and the demon that had been torturing her the last time was there as well.

There were a pair of men in the room with her, neither of which was the man who had been present yesterday. One of the visible prisoners was a muscular young man, about Patrick's size, with light brown hair and welts covering his naked body. His dark eyes were defiant, despite the bruises that covered his face. The other was much smaller, with dark blond hair and not as many welts. Sweat added a bright sheen to the smaller man's skin, and streaks of dried tears stained his cheeks.

As they watched, the demon led the smaller

man off towards an exit at the opposite end of the room.

Troy and Joel stepped up next to Todd, one on either side, and they added their own strength to Todd's, trying to push through the barrier. Even their additional strength wasn't enough to break through the mirror. Both of the hybrids started to growl in frustration and Troy scraped at the wall with his sharp fingernails. More people stepped forward, trying to push through the barrier, but to no avail. The stretchy material started to warp as the wall between the dimensions distorted.

When the demon came back into view, he no longer had the prisoner with him. He strode over to where the second man still stood, attached to a chain that hung from the ceiling behind Jen. The demon dropped the second man to the floor as well, and led him off in the same direction he had taken the previous one. As the pair moved past Jen, he spoke to her, and Todd pressed his ear to the mirror. "I think I can hear something," he said.

The others moved closer and tried to listen as well, pushing the barrier further into the next dimension. Todd swatted at the hybrids to quiet so that they could hear.

"Since they seem to be tired, it appears I will have to bring in another toy to play with," the demon explained to Jen. "Maybe Bailey is up for another round. After all, I wouldn't want to deprive him of his daily exercise."

"Leave him out of this," Jen responded, her voice almost as much of a growl as Troy's had been. "He's still bleeding from the last time you brought him out."

Todd's eyes widened in shock as he realized that Jen had started to glow. Blue and gold sparks flew off of her like fireworks, raining down over everything in the room. As the colors flew further and further from her, Todd recognized what was happening. "Jen, no!" he called out.

He looked at the rest of the group and realized that none of them could see the energy that was leaking out of her. "Get down!" He threw himself to the floor, getting down as low as he could. Around him, he could feel the rest of the group moving to lie on the floor as well.

"What's going on?" Charlie asked from somewhere behind them.

"Overload blast," Todd answered as he covered his head with his hands. "It just might tear through, so get ready."

"Oh, shit," someone exclaimed as Jen burst into electric blue flames.

The blast roared across the room she was in, rolling up the walls on the far side and searing straight through the portal that Todd still held onto. Searing heat passed over all of them and Todd hoped that the wide frame of the mirror meant that everyone was below the blast zone.

The last time he had seen a blast that powerful had been in his first year in the Academy, when one of the students had managed to explode one of the instructors' gazing balls. Todd still had a scar on his arm from the shrapnel that the explosion had caused.

That explosion, powerful as it was, had been a bottle rocket compared to the dynamite beyond the glass.

As more fire ripped through the room, Todd peeked from beneath his protective arms to confirm that the blast was almost done. The last of the explosion flowed over them and Jen lay in the middle of the blast zone, panting with the expulsion. On the ground nearby, both the demon and his prisoner were flat on the ground, scorched and singed from the detonation.

Slowly, Todd pushed himself up to his knees and swept the area with his eyes, taking a quick assessment of the situation. The rest of the group was looking around in amazement but none of them seemed to have been harmed. Toward the back of the group, David scooped up a fire extinguisher to put out a handful of small fires that had been ignited by the blast.

"What was that?" Ty asked, looking around in wonder. "Was that the demon?"

"Damn, I hope not," Marc responded, coughing a couple of times as if to accentuate everyone's discomfort. "Is it over?"

"For the moment," Todd answered as he pushed himself the rest of the way to his feet. He looked into the chamber where Jen was still chained to the bench and discovered that the broad-shouldered prisoner had wrapped his chain leash around the demon's neck and was squeezing for all he was worth. He could hear the man's panting and the sounds of screaming from somewhere further in the dark realm and reached out a tentative hand to test the barrier.

When his hand passed through with no resistance whatsoever, he jumped to his feet and scrambled into the room towards his sister, ignoring the demon for the moment.

Dealing with the demon was the team's job.

He just needed to get to his sister and get her out of there.

Chapter 14

Jen had been sound asleep when she was jolted awake by someone yanking on her leash. She was dragged across the room and would have been pulled across a couple of the other prisoners if they hadn't moved out of the way. Once she was awake enough to realize what was going on, she discovered that Cylin had come back for her already.

A small part of her had dared to hope that his abuse the day before would have satisfied him for a little bit longer but a much larger part of her realized that Cylin enjoyed the abuse more than anything else and when he had waiting victims, he couldn't wait to get his hands on them. She had also noticed that Cylin apparently lacked the mental abilities of Thaxter, the fair-haired demon and she wondered if that was a skill that he was still developing or if it was something that he simply lacked. She knew that it was also possible that he chose not to use his mental powers on them but she couldn't think of a good reason why he would do that. Since he was obviously subservient to Thaxter, it was possible that the more powerful demon had prohibited his protégé from using it.

Because of those differences, Jen almost hoped to find Thaxter waiting to play with her instead of just being entertainment for the vicious Cylin. When the demon brought her into the torture room, however, there was nobody else there. With a sigh, Jen waited for the inevitable.

Rather than hanging her from a wall as he usually did, Cylin suspended her from the trapeze. He locked her wrists to the bar and her ankles to the ground before heading back to the dark room. Jen slumped against her chains as she wondered who else would be brought to the party this time.

Cylin walked back into the torture room leading Jon on his lead. Jon crawled on his hands and knees, as all of the other prisoners did, and followed obediently along as Cylin brought him over next to where Jen already hung. While the demon was occupied attaching his ankles to the floor, Jon looked up at Jen, an expression of apology in his eyes.

Jen pursed her lips and sent him a silent kiss, widening Jon's eyes in amusement at the gesture. He barely caught himself before laughing out loud, not willing to accept the punishment of making any unwarranted sound in front of the sadistic demon. There wasn't much that Jen could do to alleviate the damage that Cylin was about to inflict on her new friend but if she could distract him for even a moment, it might make it easier on him.

Once he had Jon secured to the floor, Cylin walked out of the room again. Jen watched him leave in surprise, wondering what the bastard was up to. He almost never put more than two captives in the brightly-lit room at the same time, so she wondered what he was doing. When he came back out, however, she understood.

Little Zack crawled along behind the incubus, trying desperately to keep up with the demon's long strides. Cylin brought him over and placed him on the opposite side of Jen from Jon and shackled him in place as well. She looked down at him in horror as she realized the demon's plan. It was bad enough when he beat one of the other captives within her sight, but she had almost as soft of a spot for Zack as she had for Bailey. Somewhere along the way, the demon had figured this out and Jen winced in the realization that she had let it slip somehow. It was bad enough being beaten herself but being forced to watch others being beaten with her was even greater torture. The beatings inflicted on Bailey and Zack brought the torture to a whole new level.

Cylin tugged the wheeled cart into place and pulled down one of his favorite whips. "Now, which of you should be first?"

Jen couldn't resist. "I think I know why you like this so much."

Cylin raised an eyebrow questioningly at her and walked into position to strike her back. "And why is that?"

"Because you can't get it up on your own," she answered, and felt the responding lash across her back almost immediately. The strike was followed by more in quick succession, and she gritted her teeth to bite back a yelp. She had long since run out of creative taunts to use against the demon but she wasn't above recycled material. Particularly when that material only served to antagonize her abuser.

"You think not?" he asked as he whipped her. "Maybe I'll show you what I can get up after I'm done here." She knew she had hit a nerve with that one because he changed where he was hitting her. Now he started to aim for more sensitive places than just on her back. She bit down again and started to pull the energy from around her, knowing now that the energy was helping her to heal as quickly as she did. It didn't help much with the initial pain from each blow but it made the pain decrease as the skin closed again. She continued to insult him, spitting out every derogatory thought that came to mind, until she was too exhausted from the beating to say much of anything clever.

She could see both Jon and Zack, silently pleading with her to stop but she knew that as soon as she did, the demon would remember they were supposed to be beaten as well and she wanted to expend as much of the demon's ire as she could before that. She knew when Cylin had heard enough of her taunts because he reached up over her head and toggled a switch, dropping her and the bar she was hanging onto low enough to slam her to her knees. He walked around behind Jon and grinned at her over his shoulder and said, "He bleeds until you shut up."

"Not the first time I've heard that," Jon retorted.

Apparently the demon wasn't expecting the response from his normally docile prisoner because Cylin's eyes widened in rage. He drew his hand back and struck Jon with what seemed to be all his strength. "How dare you, you insolent brat?" He spat at Jon as he beat him mercilessly. "I would think that by now you would know better than to disobey me."

He beat Jon until the man cried out in pain before looking over at Jen. "This is your fault," the sadistic demon informed her. "I hope you are satisfied with what you have done."

Next Cylin turned his attention to Zack,

beating him every bit as mercilessly as he had done to Jon. "Think about this," he instructed Jen, including Jon in his glance, "the next time you want to defy me."

Once Zack was barely conscious from the abuse, he led the small man off to the dark room, not even bothering to hold his leash as they went. Once he was out of the room, Jon looked over at Jen. "Are you okay?"

"Yeah," she grunted in response. "A little sore, but I'll be okay soon." She looked down at him. "Why did you do that?"

He shrugged. "I don't know." He glanced over his shoulder to where the demon had disappeared into the darkness. "But I don't regret it."

"You can't keep doing that," she said. "He could've really hurt you." Her eyes darted to where the demon had disappeared with Zack. "Like he did him."

Before Jon could say anything, Cylin walked back into the room. He gave Jon a cursory examination before starting to unhook him. As he took him by the chain to lead him off, he smirked over at Jen. "Since they seem to be tired, it appears I will have to bring in another toy to play with." He led Jon a couple paces away as Jen glared at him. "Maybe Bailey is up for another round. After all, I wouldn't want to deprive him of his daily exercise."

"Leave him out of this," Jen responded, gritting her teeth as she spoke, realizing that she could feel Thaxter remotely watching the scene again. "He's still bleeding from the last time you brought him out."

"I know," the demon chuckled at her distress. "But he enjoys it so much, I doubt he'd mind."

Jen felt the energy inside of her begin to spill over as she fought to contain the rage she felt at Cylin's simple, brutal comment. It bubbled and boiled inside of her and she tried to keep it contained but it was too much for her to hold in. Blue and gold sparks fell all around and it took her a moment to realize that they were coming from her. She gritted her teeth and growled, fighting to regain control but there was no hope of success. The shower of sparks flew all over the room like a snow globe designed by a madman.

Somewhere in the distance, she could swear she heard her brother calling her name.

Fire seared through her body, burning her from the inside and when she opened her eyes, she could see bright cerulean flames dancing just under the skin of her arms. As the fires burned hotter and more fiercely, licks of bright azure flame burst out through her skin and shot across the room.

She closed her eyes against the assault. Every wave of fire that tore across the room had ripped out of her body and she tried to bite down to keep from screaming in agony but her body refused to cooperate. She clenched every muscle, tightening her hands into fists and pulling so tightly against her restraints that she could feel her skin tear. Blood, cooler than the fires that still raged around her, dripped in fine lines towards the floor.

Instinctively she knew that if she didn't regain control soon, she wouldn't survive. The fires inside of her were threatening to tear her apart and she could feel herself straining to stay intact. It took every ounce of strength and concentration she had but she slowly felt the pain begin to subside. She knew that she had gained some control over the energy but she didn't know how long it would last.

In the next room, she could hear the other prisoners screaming. She knew that they were scared and she didn't blame them but there was nothing she could do at the moment to alleviate their fear. On the floor nearby, Cylin had been knocked flat by the wave of energy. He lay sprawled on the floor, only inches away from Jon. At first, Jen thought they were both dead because neither of them was moving but then Jon groaned and pushed himself up onto his hands. He looked around, eyes wide at the damage she had wrought but as Cylin started to move also, he rolled towards the demon.

Using the same chain that the demon had been using moments ago as a leash, Jon wrapped Cylin's neck tightly, his muscles bulging with exertion. He snarled and growled with the effort and Jen could see that his face was turning red from the strain. Cylin's face was changing color as well, from the light tan that he had always had to a deep purple as his prisoner-turned-assailant stopped the airflow.

Suddenly, from out of nowhere, men rushed into the room. They were shouting among themselves and aiming weapons in all directions. One of them moved immediately to Jen's side and only then did she recognize her brother. "Todd?" she breathed, not sure if he was really there or just a figment of her imagination.

"Yeah, just hold still a minute. I'm going to get you off this thing." He reached down to try and release the cuffs that attached her wrists to the bench but the strange locks refused to yield. He looked around the room, and Jen followed his glance.

The rest of her team was there, as were Troy, Patrick, and Joel alongside another man she didn't recognize. The hybrids were trying to wrest Cylin away from Jon but he was obviously confused and not willing to release the demon.

"Jon," she called over to him. When he looked up and met her eyes, she nodded. "Let go. They're friends."

Jon looked doubtful but he relinquished his suffocating hold on the demon. As Cylin gasped for air, the hybrids descended on him like the pack of wolves from which they had descended.

"Do you know how to open these locks?" Todd called over to him. When Jon nodded, the mage gestured him over. "Help me get her out of here."

Jon rolled to his knees and crawled over towards them. Jen wasn't sure if he was crawling because of the damage that the demon had done to his legs or if it was because he wasn't sure if she was going to explode again but it didn't matter. Once he was at her side, he showed Todd how to release the locks.

Todd helped her to sit up and pulled off his shirt to cover her. "You're okay now; we've got you." He looked at the welts that were quickly fading from her skin, being careful not to accidentally brush against any of them. As he looked down at her, he realized that no matter where he touched her, he was going to come into contact with one of them.

"We need to get the others out," Jen explained as Todd lifted her up off the bench after she and Jon finished freeing her legs. She grimaced as she pulled Todd's shirt over her head, stretching the collar out to fit more easily without scraping the tender skin. "We can't just leave them here."

A strange look crossed Todd's face. "The portal will only hold ten people. I don't have enough power to open it any wider than that."

"Then take mine," she answered, her voice weak. "I don't want to risk losing control of it like that again."

The snarling hybrids still had Cylin pinned to the ground but it seemed that the demon felt like fighting back. He thrashed and kicked out at the hybrids, landing a foot squarely in Troy's groin. The blow knocked the hybrid backwards but Joel simply wrapped his long legs around the demon's body, wrapped his arms around Cylin's legs, and pushed out with a foot, stretching the demon out to his full length.

"Hey!" Ty called over to the rest of the group. He stood at the doorway that led to the holding cell. "We've got more people over here!"

"How many?" Marc called over.

Ty shrugged. "I can't tell, but there's a lot."

Jen looked up at Todd beseechingly. "We have to help them." She tried to move and stand on her own but her legs wouldn't support her. She collapsed against her brother, who clasped her tightly against his side. She hissed in pain as he pressed against her welts but the hot pain was secondary to her insistence that she wasn't going to leave the other prisoners behind.

"I'll get them," Jon offered. In obvious pain, he stood and Jen smiled up at him in gratitude. "Can someone help me with them, though?" he asked. "I'm pretty sure that Zack isn't going to be able to walk and there are a couple of others who are pretty badly hurt, too."

Patrick stepped closer to him. "I can help too." He looked over at Todd and Jen. "You guys okay for the moment?" When Jen indicated they were, he turned to Jon and nodded. As they headed for the dark room, Ty and J.J. joined them to help retrieve the rest of the captives.

Troy growled as he stood back up and he slowly stepped closer to the struggling pair. As he stepped over the demon, he growled something unintelligible down to his friend, who grunted and stretched the demon further. Troy leaned down, growling and snarling, and buried both of his thumbs, sharpened nails first, into the demon's throat.

Cylin's scream of pain turned into a gurgle as his blood spilled out of the gaping wound in his throat. Joel released his hold on him and he and Troy hoisted the dying demon to his feet and dragged him to the closest wall, where Joel pinned him to the floor again. Troy grabbed a wall sconce and bent it outwards. As soon as he stepped back away from it, Joel lifted Cylin and hung him from the light fixture. Troy bent the metal bars up again to secure the demon in place.

While the hybrids were busy, Ty and J.J. walked into the room leading a group of prisoners that they had released. Each of them was carrying one of the most damaged ones and Jen choked back a sob as she recognized Bailey, barely conscious from his wounds, in Ty's grasp. Dried blood was caked on his skin and his bruises were still an angry purple from the beating he had received the previous night.

Jon led more of them out, his arms wrapped around Christy as she tried to walk on her own. She was still covered in welts and bruises from the sadistic demons, bruises covered the areas that weren't already swollen from the lash.

Patrick came out soon afterwards, carrying a frightened and crying Zack. It looked like the small man didn't realize that he was being rescued, and he was still in too much pain to do much but cling to Patrick and allow himself to be taken away. When he recognized Jon standing nearby, he relaxed some, but he still whimpered in pain with every step Patrick took.

Although Jen hadn't noticed, Mike and the new man must have followed the trio into the holding cell because they came out helping more people. "I think that's all of them," Mike explained once everyone was out.

Todd looked uncertainly down at Jen, who he still held tight against him. "Are you sure about this?" he asked. When Jen nodded, he pointed out, "It'll probably hurt."

"I don't care," she answered. "I can't leave them behind."

"Okay then." Todd walked her over to the bulge between worlds. Though the portal was still visible, the opening had closed quickly after allowing the team to pass through. He pulled his sister in even tighter and took her arm in his hand to raise it up. "Aim for there," he instructed her.

Jen felt the power rise in her again but this time it wasn't the raging inferno it had been before. She closed her eyes and relaxed, trusting in her brother's guidance. Like a geyser, the energy erupted out of her towards the thin veil that barred them from going home. This time, unlike the previous, the fire was more gold than blue and it washed over the portal and burned through it, creating a hole that was easily twice as large as the one Todd had created.

"Go," Todd shouted to the group. "We'll follow you out."

Joel and Troy moved forward but instead of leading the way through the doorway like Jen had thought they were, they stopped on either side of her, as though they were standing guard.

Jon, on the other hand, needed no further encouragement. He tightened his grip on Christy and headed for the doorway. As he stepped through it, he faded from view. Ty and J.J. followed suit, carrying people with them as well and leading more out of the demonic world.

Soon everyone made it safely back to the other side and Todd sent the hybrids through as well. With one last glance over his shoulder at the demon's lifeless body, he carried his sister home.

Chapter 15

As Thaxter opened the front door of his house, he could feel that there was something wrong. He stepped inside, expecting to be greeted by the enthusiastic sounds of Cylin at work but there was only silence.

Slowly, he crept through the house towards the playroom, wondering why everything was quiet and hoping that Cylin was merely taking a break. He had already lost Vanitha and he wasn't sure where her protégé had run off to after her capture, so all he had left was Cylin and his group of play things.

He pushed the door to the playroom, letting it swing open on its well-oiled hinges and stepped across the storage area towards the entertainment chamber. He stopped in the doorway, stunned at the carnage he found there.

Everything looked as though it had been burned; scorch marks covered the floor and crept halfway up his expensive stone walls. His tool cart had been knocked over and his prized collection of whips had been stepped on and burned as well. It was obvious that Cylin had been using the leather bench, no surprise since it was one of his favorite pieces of furniture. Now, however, the leather was dried and cracked and it looked as though it had been set on fire as well. There was the shape of a body in relief on the bench, as though whoever had been strapped to it had taken the brunt of the fire but the bench was destroyed nevertheless.

Loose chains and a handful of hastily removed collars indicated that the slaves may have initiated a revolt but Thaxter doubted it. Some of them had been his loyal playthings for too long to even consider staging any type of resistance and he couldn't imagine any of the slaves being able to overpower Cylin, particularly considering the amount of damage each of the slaves had received over the last few days.

That thought stopped him as he realized that there was one particular plaything that may have possessed the ability to do this. One of his newest, the last one gifted to him by Vanitha before she was captured, had developed the ability to draw the energy that he and Cylin had spent so much effort cultivating. If she had figured out how to use it, there was a very real possibility that she could have escaped.

The demon stepped through the mess towards the slaves' chamber. Inside, he had expected to find a handful of his less loyal toys missing but he hadn't expected to find them all gone. He felt the irritation build inside him as he looked around the dark room and he sensed that the one called Jen hadn't been the only one here taking them away from him. The stink of werewolf permeated the air all around him and he wondered if her half-breed friends had come after her.

When he stepped back into the entertainment chamber, he stopped short at what he saw. When he had initially entered the room, he hadn't been in a position to see what the filthy mutts had done to his protégé. He stepped over the ruined pieces of his livelihood and took Cylin's face in his hand, lifting his chin to look into the lesser demon's sightless eyes.

He had been beaten severely, as evidenced by the bruises and welts that covered large portions of his body. The fire that had damaged the play room had done a number on Cylin as well, as his black hair smelled burnt and was a good deal shorter than it once had been. Marks from where he had been choked by a chain stood in bright contrast on the thin skin of the demon's neck, broken only by the pair of puncture holes that still continued to ooze blood, one last detail that declared how he had suffered before his death.

"It appears that you were not a good choice to leave here guarding them after all," he said to his onetime student. As he turned to walk out of the room, he debated on what to do about the latest change in an already difficult situation.

"Who is going to keep her from the Inquisitors now?"

Keep reading for an exclusive sneak peek at

Mind Games

Available October, 2024

Sneak Peek

"You know they're going to get the court order sooner or later," Marc pointed out to the other two as he paced. "Todd's got them held at bay for the moment but we all know that won't last long."

"Like I told you," Charlie turned his head to watch the pacing man, "if they were going to get a court order, they would have done it by now."

"I know," Marc said, "but now they want to bring in some sort of a specialist to see her? It's only a matter of time before they get their stooge to say she needs more than North Bank can provide. With their doctor in their corner, it won't matter what Todd says, they'll just take her anyway."

Charlie shook his head. "Greg's a good guy; he wouldn't do something like that." He looked down at the cup of coffee on the desk in front of him. He picked it up to take a drink but its contents had long since gone cold and he put it back down again. "That's why I asked him to take this case."

Marc stopped pacing and looked at him incredulously. "You asked for this?" He stepped closer to the seated man, incensed. "How could you do that?"

"Because she needs it, which you know every bit as well as I do," David interrupted. "You need to calm down, Marc." When Marc scowled but stopped pacing, David continued. "As far as I'm concerned, the argument over who is treating Jen is irrelevant. Our main concern should be for her and that she is getting treatment she needs so that she can get better. The doctors who had been treating her are still there and Dr. McAdam has agreed to keep them in the loop on what's happening with her and they are keeping us updated as well."

"Updates are nice but why hasn't she woken up yet? It's almost been a week."

"Think about it," Charlie said. "That girl just went through hell, quite literally. It's not really much of a surprise if she needs a break to process it all." He looked over at Marc and continued. "It's actually pretty common after a heavy trauma like what she went through."

Marc shook his head. "All of the others that we brought back with her are awake. Hell, most of them have already been released from the hospital and taken to that group home they're staying in."

"Exactly," Charlie said. "But Jen still isn't awake, so having a psychic come in to treat her is the best option for her right now. Like David said, our focus is on getting her better. The rest can be dealt with if and when it happens." He picked up his cup and poured more hot coffee into it to warm it up again.

"But will she wake up?"

"When she's ready to. Like I said, it's not unusual for someone's mind to turn off for a bit when they've been through something traumatic. It gives them a chance to sort through everything and not have to deal with all of the outside crap while they're accepting what happened." He took another drink of his coffee. "Frankly, I'd be more worried if she hadn't shut down. That would mean that she isn't really dealing with what happened yet and she's more likely to have an emotional breakdown over it later, when it finally sinks in what happened."

"So you're saying this is actually good for her." When Charlie nodded, Marc thought for another moment. "Has your doctor found anything yet?"

David picked up a stapled packet of papers from his desk. "The report I got said that Dr. McAdam hasn't found anything physically wrong with her yet. He's been monitoring her own healing rate and keeping track of what she's doing to herself while she's asleep. She's still making some small adjustments but nothing too major, it looks like."

Before Marc could ask any more questions, the phone on David's desk started to ring. He picked it up, mildly irritated at the interruption, but his attitude swiftly changed. "That's great news, thanks for calling. Yes, we're on our way right now."

He hung up the phone and looked over at the other two men as he stood up and reached for his jacket. "That was the hospital. Jen just woke up."

Marc grinned for the first time since Jen had been taken. "It's about damn time," he said as he headed for the door. "A nap's one thing but this is pushing it a little."

Even Charlie snickered as they stepped into the elevator. "I wouldn't recommend saying that in front of her," he said. "From what I've heard, she's liable to beat you with one of the flower arrangements her sister brought down for her."

Marc thought about that. "You've got a point," he conceded and looked at David. "Do we have time for me to grab my body armor before we go?"

After life growing up in the beautifully rainy Pacific Northwest, Shanon L. Mayer tends to keep indoors, writing story after story, building vivid worlds on paper while her thoughts hold everything but images. She tends to look at everything in her world for inspiration – especially her collections of skulls, dragon statues, swords and knives, and pretty much anything that fits her eclectic, geeky-gothic lifestyle.

When her busy life feels like too much, she can be found relaxing with a hot mug of tea and a documentary on anything from theoretical physics to deep ocean wildlife to the most famous heists the world has ever seen.